# Timothy Cratchit's Christmas Carol, 1917

## Dale Powell
For speaking or teaching engagements, call 1-888-750-4802
or write PO Box 585, Lucasville, OH 45648

An original story based on characters created by
## Charles Dickens (1812-1870)

ISBN 1-893069-02-8

Printed in USA

Copyright 1998 by Dale K. Powell. All rights reserved. Published by
DickensWorld.

DickensWorld is a pending registered trademark.

No part of this publication may be reproduced in part or whole by any means without written permission of the publisher, excepting brief excerpts for review or scholarly purposes not done for profit.

First printing, September 1998

Printed in Arkansas City, Kansas, USA

*Dedicated to:*

*My boys, Nathan and Shawn*

*My wife, Barbara*

*A great friend, Nathan Burton*

*The New Thought Unity Center in Cincinnati, Ohio*

*The memory and work of Charles Dickens*

*Elsie Shabazz, of Portsmouth, Ohio, who in many ways was my inspiration in creating the character of Elsie Brown.*


*Special thanks to:*

*My brother, Rick Powell, for cover design, web design, editorial work and encouragement.*

*My brother, Mark Powell, for technical Internet assistance.*

*Chris Woodyard (author of* Haunted Ohio *series) for publishing advice.*

The Beginning of It All......................

from *A Christmas Carol,* by Charles Dickens, 1843

Scrooge was better than his word. He did it all and infinitely more; and to Tiny Tim, **<u>who did not die,</u>** he was a second father. He became as good a friend, as good a master, and as good a man, as the good old city knew...........

Some people laughed to this alteration in him, but he let them laugh and heeded them little.............

...it was said of him that he knew how to keep Christmas well, if any man alive possessed the knowledge. May that truly be said of all of us. And so, as Tiny Tim (Cratchit) observed, God Bless Us, Every One!

Foreword

A sequel to Dickens? What kind of arrogant writer takes it upon himself to write a sequel to the work of one of the greatest novelists of all time? And to one of his best known works at that?

Charles Dickens was born in Portsmouth, England in 1812. In 1962-one hundred fifty years later- I was born in Portsmouth, Ohio. Coincidence? Yes, I'm sure it is. Other than the fact that we both share a partiality to children and to Christmas, that is where the similarities end.

Dickens was a great writer. I have a lot of good ideas, but I am not a Dickens. He was a natural; I have to work hard.

Having acknowledged my shortcomings to the master, please allow me a moment to explain my purpose in writing this follow up to what I consider quite possibly the greatest story ever written. As a teacher, I am an inquiring mind. Dickens tells us that Tiny Tim Cratchit did not die, so he must have lived, right? How ? Did he follow in his father's footsteps and become a clerk? Where did he live? Did he have a family? Did he appreciate the difference in the life of his father's early years to his good fortune in having Ebeneezer Scrooge as a second father?

I have explored that realm into a logical pattern of events that would lead Timothy Cratchit to Christmas Eve, 1917 in Cincinnati, Ohio. Having overcome Scrooge's demon of greed and self-centeredness, Cratchit is plagued with a poverty of the spirit when World War I deals him a devastating blow.

May you and your family enjoy *Timothy Cratchit's Christmas Carol 1917*. If its message is only a fraction as well received as Dickens' original, it will have been worth my time to have written it, as well as yours for reading it. *God bless us, everyone!*

# Stave One - Nothing Lasts Forever

  Christmas Eve, 1917, arrived on the calendar in the parlor of Timothy Cratchit's stately Cincinnati manor, but the occasion failed to reach his heart. The Great War, the one that found the British born octogenarian watching his native land and his adopted home of America claiming to fight the imperialism of the aggressor nations, had dealt Cratchit the cruelest of blows. No merriment presided in his heart; it was only December 24, 1917.

  All the newspapers called it the Great War. Those two words- great and war- should never be in the same sentence, but yet that is the herald that the press had chosen for it. No matter what it was called, it bore in Cratchit's mind as only murder most foul, and though the killing was taking place thousands of miles from the banks of the Ohio River, Cratchit swore he could smell the waters bringing its stench.

  Nevertheless, Timothy Cratchit modeled the look of a gentleman, and he would have appeared so on either side of the Atlantic. Dressed in a tan pinstriped suit, Cratchit could have passed for twenty less than his eighty-one years. Though not a terribly lofty man, he still stood tall with a gold chain adorning the outer pocket of his vest. His only outward trace of wear was seen in a slight limp which had resurfaced only recently from a birth defect, his silver hair, and the lines of his face that seemed to deepen only over the past few weeks.

  Until that time, Cratchit could still be seen often strolling the Cincinnati neighborhood where he lived. He had long outgrown the childhood title "Tiny Tim", which was bestowed upon him affectionately as a lad in London due to his frailty as a youth and his diminutive stature.

Though wearing its holiday fineries, the city still pervaded in a dismal despair of war. Tinsel and candles do not erase the images of gunfire that was told to be raging by land, sea and air. Air travel- which Cratchit had proclaimed only a year or so ago to be the miracle of the age had robbed him of his last reason for which the old widower had wanted to live. His beloved Luke, the only son of his only son had fallen victim to the monster, the War of the World.

The message still lay on the desk in his parlor.

\*\*\*\*\*\*\*\*\*\*\*\*\*\*\*\*\*\*\*\*\*\*\*\*\*\*\*\*\*\*\*\*\*\*\*\*\*\*\*\*\*\*\*\*\*\*\*\*\*\*\*\*\*\*\*\*

*Young Luke Jacob Cratchit was just nineteen years of age the day he entered his grandfather's Vine Street office. His face was aglow that spring afternoon with a look of urgency that still carried with it a certain expectation, if not eagerness for an adventure.*

*"Grandfather, it's a fact; the States are joining in the war! President Wilson said that it can't be avoided any longer," Luke had announced to his grandfather.*

*The old man had turned to his grandson without his general gladsome look in his eye. With a wisdom that seems reserved for the aged, Timothy Cratchit gazed a lengthy sincere look at his grandson, but gave no reply. Timothy had heard the President's address on the radio and was grimly aware of what consequences it held for his family.*

*"Guess I'll be going back over to Europe before you do, Grandfather. I'll probably even be in England, although I more*

than likely won't get to look up our kinsmen," the younger Cratchit speculated.

Still, the old man stared at his grandson. The boy was so handsome and the old man loved him so much that even in these dismal circumstances he found himself smiling.

Rising, Timothy Cratchit stretched his arms to hug the youth. "Luke," he said gladly, his smile hiding a few tears. "Luke."

Stating his beloved grandchild's name was the only words his eighty-one year old lips could form at this point. The two shared a long, masculine embrace that Timothy finally broke apart to hold his grandson firmly by both shoulders and continue his admiring gaze at the young man.

Finally, Luke found the words to speak. "Grandfather, we've known it for some time. It was bound to happen. You've said so yourself."

"Yes," came the reply from Timothy as he held his grandson against his breast.

Staring blindly at the wall behind him while his grandfather continued the hearty embrace, Luke replied, "I'll just be going to Europe a little before you, Grandfather. And," he added off handedly, "you won't be traveling with me as we had planned."

Timothy Cratchit was resigned. He began, "Things . . . things will not be as planned, Luke. I know it's pointless to ask you not to go . . ."

"It's best that I go now," Luke began, "if I wait, there will be conscription and I'll get the worst assignments..."

His explanation was cut short by his grandfather's acknowledging nod. Luke was repeating to his grandfather the words that the old man had stated to him when talk of the United States entry into the war was mere speculation. Cratchit's native

England had long been besieged with the fighting, and Cratchit was glad to be living in the United States of America.

The election banners of 1916 touted President Woodrow Wilson as the hero who had kept us out of war. Cratchit remembered vividly; "He kept us out of war," the Democratic rally posters proclaimed. It was the deciding factor that had caused Cratchit to vote for the president.

Remembering was pointless.

"I'll be fine, Grandfather," said Luke reassuringly. "Then when the war is over and its safe to travel, we can take that trip back to London."

"I'll never see London again." Timothy Cratchit's answer was as cold as it was convincing. The conviction of the old man's heart gave his voice a tone of finality that made Luke think of not only his own, but also his Grandfather's mortality.

"The war can't last forever, Grandfather."

The older Cratchit sat resolutely for a moment, then asked, "Can't it?"

\*\*\*\*\*\*\*\*\*\*\*\*\*\*\*\*\*\*\*\*\*\*\*\*\*\*\*\*\*\*\*\*\*\*\*\*\*\*\*\*\*\*\*\*\*\*\*\*\*\*\*\*\*\*\*

Like a stone it lay there.

Regaining his thoughts as he stood staring at the message on this particular day, Christmas Eve, Cratchit involuntarily stated aloud, "A war can last forever."

"Excuse me, Mr. Cratchit?" asked a voice from the next room. The sound now presented itself in the form of female, pleasant enough to behold in her uniformed attire of a maid. The articulation was that of Elsie, Timothy Cratchit's housekeeper.

"Something I can help you with, Mr. Cratchit?" Elsie asked with a genuine pleasantness that allowed one to instantly get a glimpse of the resplendent soul that Cratchit's African-American housekeeper possessed.

For a moment, Cratchit stood and stared blankly. Fearing an urgency with the old man's health, Elsie rushed to him.

"Mr. Cratchit, are you all right, sir?" she implored.

Back to the present moment, Cratchit smiled faintly and nodded.

She walked over to him. "It's O.K. to think about Master Luke. I still keep thinking he'll be coming in this Christmas Eve like always. Then I catch myself and realize that he's not coming in and Zebulon isn't coming either."

Elsie's brother, Zebulon, had fallen victim to the war only a month before word of Luke's tragedy reached Cincinnati.

"Times are different now, Elsie," Timothy said solemnly. "Things end. But this damned old war, and what it's done to Luke, and your brother, that's permanent. That's where it ends for them."

"The love I feel for my brother isn't dead, Mr. Cratchit. Just like the love we both feel for young Master Luke. That won't ever die, sir. Nothing can ever kill that." Elsie fixed her eyes upon the employer she had grown to love as a father. Socioeconomic and racial differences had no bearing on their relationship. Each had a mutual respect for the other that transcended any classification that human minds can assign.

Cratchit began, "I'm waiting for my grave now, Elsie; there's nothing left for me to do now. I've attempted to live-I've had my share of good fortune. But time, like the thief that it is, has found me and stolen what was left of my place on earth. It's over now."

Elsie placed her soft hand to the face of her benefactor. "It's not over. God sees fit for you to be. My family and I- we need you, Mr. Cratchit. And you know me well enough to know I'm not talking about money. Yes, I need this job, but my family needs you. Part of my family is you!"

"Now, it's Christmas, and I know that can always bring anybody mixed emotions, but dwelling on the bad isn't what Christmas is all about."

"Christmas," Cratchit began, "Christmas. I guess I've derived all the good that I ever will from this life. And that good life does include many a Christmas, Elsie. Oh when I was a boy in London, my mother and father were poor, our family was large and for quite a time I was very ill, but we did celebrate Christmas."

"Yes, Mr. Cratchit. See, you can still smile. Benjamin and the kids are really looking forward to your coming over tomorrow and then..."

Cratchit cut Elsie short of finishing her comments. "I won't be over tomorrow, Elsie."

The conversation paused for only a beat when Elsie began upbraiding her boss. "Now, Mr. Cratchit, you must not shut down just because..." Unfortunately, the housekeeper let emotion over take her intellect and she found herself at a loss for words."

"You were saying, Elsie? Something like, just because my last living relative on this continent returned to my homeland to be slaughtered in a senseless war? Elsie, the facts are that my life before the war no longer exists. My family's not the same, Cincinnati's not the same, the world's not the same! My physician of twenty-two years sneaks in and out of my house at dusk to avoid being seen in my company by his kinsmen. There's one thing left for me to do, Elsie, and that's not found in the celebration of

Christmas. The only thing left for me to do is die. I'm just waiting for the Creator to take me, and I wish he'd be quick about it."

Elsie stood, her head hung, not daring to look at the old man. The tongue that had helped earn Cratchit his wealth through business transactions was a jackal that Elsie did not want to fight. She loved the old man; seeing him hurt pierced her heart.

And there were certainly parts of his arguments that to which she could not lay a denial. Nothing was the same. Aside from the tragedies that had touched both of their families, the city found itself in an internal struggle. Being a city that found its greatest growth in immigrants, Cincinnati was home to thousands of British immigrants like Cratchit, but also to a host of German descendants. This had deeply divided the Queen City, watching street signs that had long born German names renamed something more "English" or "American". Dr. Strauss, Cratchit's long time friend and physician had dropped most of his non-German patients. This was not due to any prejudice felt on the part of the doctor, but rather to avoid the scorn of his own community. For Cratchit, though, he risked the ridicule; he would stop in to see the old man from time to time on his way home from his office. Elsie would let the physician in the back door so that he did not have to risk being viewed entering the home of a known Englishman from the street.

Finally thinking of something to say, the housekeeper put her arms around the old man from behind him and said, "There's a lot of good left in you, Mr. Cratchit. I know who made that large anonymous donation to the Children's Orphanage Society, and I know who it is helping the war widows around here too. And I sure know who it is that puts the presents under my family's Christmas tree."

"I have a lot of money, Elsie. I'm just giving back what has been generously given to me by God. But I'm of no value to anyone anymore. When I'm gone, they can have all of my money. Dead! That's what I need to be, and that's all I'm waiting for. That's the way that I can be of the most service to humanity."

"I don't believe that, Timothy Robert Cratchit. You are one of the finest men God has put on this earth. He has seen fit to share you with two different centuries and two continents, and by the looks of your health, he's not through with you yet."

"Well, then I wish he'd be quick about it. Luke should be here; I should be dead." He spoke with the authority of a judge. His words were heavy stones that left indentations where they struck.

"It's Christmas, Mr. Cratchit. That used to mean something to you, sir."

Cratchit looked through her and out the window. "What used to be doesn't count any more, Elsie."

Again at a loss for words, the housekeeper left the parlor as the old man sat in his familiar chair of fine leather. His gaze was fixed, but blank and pointless. After a moment, he picked up the formidable message, and read again as if for the first time. When he came to the part that told of Luke's death, a single tear fell down Timothy Cratchit's weathered cheek.

■■■■■■■■■■■■■■■■■■■■■■■■■■■■■■■■■■■■■■■■■■■■■■■■■■■■

The last day that Timothy had laid eyes upon his grandson stuck out in his memory as the most perfect spring day that he had ever seen on two continents. What a bitter contrast this setting painted with respect to the grim reality that lay ahead. Luke, as he always did, beamed a great smile when he greeted his grandfather that morning in the family dining room.

"Grandfather, how old was I when I was last in Europe?" the younger Cratchit inquired.

Pausing a moment to think, the elder Cratchit began, "It would have been- let's see- in aught-nine*, and you were born in ninety-seven, so that would have made you twelve, I suppose. Yes, you've lived with me since you were eleven and we went back to London for a visit the following year after your father and mother died."

Luke sat thoughtfully for a moment. "It's been nine years, Grandfather, but I still remember them. It's like I've never lost them; it's as if they're still on that trip, and just haven't come back."

Turning to his grandfather, he asked, "How did you go on, Grandfather? I've heard that it's much harder to lose a child, even harder than losing a parent, but you kept going. How did you do it?"

"Luke, there isn't a day that goes by that I don't think about your father and your mother, too, for I loved her as well. Similarly, I think of your grandmother. She's been gone twenty-two years, before you were born, and I still sometimes raise my voice to speak to her as if she was in the next room. It's as though they are here- sometimes I can feel their presence. You never knew your Grandmother, Luke, but I can see her alive in you. Her warmth, that smile, that blonde hair."

Timothy Cratchit laughed and ruffled his grandson's mane.

"People say that I'm a lot like father," Luke replied, "and you."

---

*aught nine – Cratchit is referring to 1909. Aught is an old American and English slang term meaning "nothing".

11

"You've got a loving heart. Like your father, Ebeneezer Cratchit, and my father, Bob Cratchit, and your mother, and grandmother, and Uncle Ebeneezer Scrooge."

"Uncle Ebeneezer Scrooge? You named your only son after him and not yourself."

"That's right, although really he wasn't my uncle, more like a second father, I guess you would say. We were kindred only in a spiritual sense. But never a kinder man ever lived. I owe my very life to him. He took an interest in me when I was but a lad in London. He had no family, but did he ever adopt us. My father said that I was deteriorating quickly, and I was likely not to see an eighth year if not for Ebeneezer Scrooge. He sought out the finest doctors in London and we even traveled to Paris for some treatment, but I got well, and all thanks to a lot of prayer, loving parents, and Mr. Ebeneezer Scrooge. I named my only son after him. Your father. And at Christmas? My, no children in England were more spoiled, and my mother used to fret over it so. But I think the truth of the matter was that she enjoyed seeing us indulged. Though she claimed that the Lord Mayor of London's own children never made merry so!"

Remembering him makes you so happy, Grandfather. He must have been quite a man, this Mr. Scrooge," Luke observed.

"One of a kind. I wish I had been more like him."

Your gentle narrator wishes to remind the kind reader that this is the impression of Ebeneezer Scrooge Mr. Dickens left with us. It has been our cynical, unforgiving minds which perennially casts him as an eternal stingy miser.

"Not I, Grandfather," came Luke's reassuring reply. "I wouldn't have you any other way than just the way you are."

"It's kind of you to say so, Luke."

"Not kind, it's true. There could be no better parent, in Cincinnati or London, than you have been to me, Grandfather."

The old man sat a moment in thought. "The only consolation that I received in losing your parents came in the fact that it allowed me to get to really know you, Luke. Oh, I loved you before, but you were a continent away, and our visits were few. Oh, how you have added life to these years, Luke. And. . . and I am going to miss you."

The grimness of the moment had returned. Luke and his grandfather would separate today.

Neither spoke of the grave possibility that lie ahead; it was not necessary to do so. Luke Jacob Cratchit would leave today to join in the service of his country in the Great World War. That is all they knew at that moment, at least on a conscious level. Somehow, Timothy Cratchit seemed to know more.

He had known more when his son and daughter left New York aboard a luxury cruise vessel bound for an around the world cruise-one of the first of its kind. The famous Titanic had sunk four years after the Cratchit's were killed, so he had no rational reason to fear the journey on which they were embarking. But still, Timothy had held his son and daughter-in-law close to him with a sense of urgency when they left, though he knew not why. He accredited it only to sensing his own mortality and fearing that he would not be able to care for their young son until their safe return.

But they never returned. Without the bannering headlines that would later accompany the Titanic disaster, Ebeneezer and

*Catherine Cratchit were among only six who perished in an explosion aboard the cruise. Several others were injured in the ordeal, but only those who were instant casualties succumbed to their injuries; the remainder survived and made it to safety aboard lifeboats.*

*Timothy Cratchit had known; he knew even before he got the official news that raising Luke had fallen upon his elderly shoulders.*

*The boy did remarkably well with his Grandfather, even flourishing under his guidance. Timothy knew that he would not let anything happen to Luke.*

*He knew.*

*But how could he stop this? Luke's country had called him to duty. Timothy Cratchit decided to ignore any extrasensory perception and enjoy his final earthly hours with his adored grandson.*

*They had some time before his departure which was scheduled to be shortly before noon. They strolled around the grounds of the stately manor, contouring many a hill and plateau, until the younger Cratchit insisted his grandfather rest. In fact, Timothy was tired. He had done quite a bit of walking and talking this morning, particularly for an eighty-one year old man. But nothing was going to take these moments from him.*

*When at last the time drew near for them to make it to the train station for Luke's departure, Timothy instructed Sloane, his driver, that he wished to take the horse and carriage today. They had a motor car, but the splendor of the spring day and his earnest desire to hold on to this moment forever, made his choice for a simpler mode of transportation desirable.*

Elsie had prepared a bountiful brunch for grandfather and grandson. Luke ate heartily, although Timothy had very little appetite. After the two had warm and sometimes tender conversation, Elsie discarded her role as maid and housekeeper to step into the part of family matriarch. She was, after all, the closest thing Luke had to a mother now.

"Miss Elsie, the thing I'm going miss the most are these biscuits," Luke began holding up a fine example of Elsie's culinary art. " Ma'am, I've found your secret. You sold your soul to the devil for the ability to create sinfully delicious food on earth." A sly grin fixed upon the face of the youth as he awaited the scorn that was sure to be sent his way.

"Luke Jacob Cratchit, you cut out that trash talk now before I send you off with a sore behind and spoonful of soap in your mouth," came the expected retort.

Timothy Cratchit smiled and interceded on behalf of his grandson, never completely sure of what the feisty, though loving, Elsie would do. "I believe," the elder Cratchit began, "that Elsie's touch has more of a heavenly flavor to it." He hoped his intercession would tame the wrath of the stern maternal side of his housekeeper to the more benevolent, affectionate one.

"That's all I meant, Miss Elsie," explained Luke in a non-authentic, worried voice. "I just meant that your cooking talents are not of this world."

Elsie gazed a hard stare upon him, stone-faced, until all three faces exploded into laughter.

The maid hugged the handsome lad and began speaking, "It isn't going to be the same with your ornery self gone from here, Master Luke." The embrace continued for many minutes.

In a more serious tone, Luke softly said, "Just for a while, Elsie. A war can't last forever."

She placed her hands squarely on both of his Luke's shoulders. "Nothing lasts forever, Luke. That's why we have minute to minute and day to day. That's why I got to tell you that I love you."

Luke seemed almost shocked by her words. It was not that the boy did not know this, but it was the manner in which she said it. There was an intensity to it that evades description.

"I love you too, Elsie."

"Well, I can't take that for granted anymore. And I won't, either." She turned to walk away.

"Miss Elsie," came the reply after a moment, "it won't be forever."

"Nothing lasts forever," she affirmed.

As Timothy walked into the vaulted great room of his Cincinnati estate on this particular Christmas Eve, his mind remained fixed on his grandson and now, their final moments together.

The carriage ride to the train station took twelve minutes on the busy Cincinnati streets, mixed with a fifty-fifty ratio of automobiles and buggy travel. The news of the U.S. entry into the war had frenzied the city to a peak of urgent excitement. Anti-German sentiment, which had already scourged the city, would now peak in the weeks, months, or even years that might follow. Most Americans were of the opinion that with the entry of the USA in the fighting, the battle would be brief. Timothy Cratchit was unconvinced. Being a native Briton, he knew first hand what the rest only knew via the newspapers. The fighting had torn Europe since 1914; it was now 1917. The magnitude of this war was unprecedented.

Luke Cratchit's ever enthusiastic view of life dimmed only slightly on the solemn carriage ride. Timothy watched the boy in silence as he saw in the youth a look that he first mistook for that of his wife. Then Timothy reasoned that he observed the look of Luke's father. As they made the final right turn before reaching the train depot, Timothy realized that he saw his own eyes, his own face, and no doubt, his own thoughts. Luke was a part of him; the two of them were truly one.

The part of Timothy that he loved the most was returning to Europe. But it was not by choice; this would be no pleasure cruise.

Too soon, the destination arrived. Sloane opened the carriage door and the two disembarked. Retrieving the bag containing the few personal items that Luke had been instructed to take with him until he received government issue, the driver walked two paces behind the two as they made their way to the departure gate.

The two seated themselves on a bench to chat the final twenty minutes-this had been their plan in arriving a little early. However, within moments of their arrival, a tall, middle-aged porter approached them and spoke directly to Luke.

"Recruit?" asked the porter.

"Yes, sir," Luke replied.

"You are to board immediately at Gate 3," the porter spoke systematically.

Timothy Cratchit spoke up at this point. "According to the papers we received from the government, Luke is to depart at 11:35. It's barely thirteen minutes past the hour."

"Sir, the war effort is of unprecedented urgency. I have been instructed to round up the recruits as soon as they arrive in an effort to get them to their destination as quickly as possible so that the train may return to pick up more needed recruits. The railroad

*has been instructed to tighten the lines to maximum capacity plus twenty-five. Indeed nearly all recruits are already aboard the train." Turning to Luke, he inquired, "Name?"*
*His reply was quick, "Luke Jacob Cratchit, sir."*
*"Gate three, immediately," came the staunch reply as the porter strolled off.*
*"Looks like goodbye, Grandfather,"*
*"I love you, Luke. You're part of who I am, son."*
*Luke's only reply was to enfold his grandfather in his arms.*
*"I want more time! I want more time with you, Luke." Timothy said with clenched teeth. In his lifetime, he had been very poor and very rich, but had definitely spent the majority of his years financially secure, able to buy whatever he desired. This is not to say that he squandered his money, and indeed he was quite generous. But he found him unable to buy more time with his son at the point of his death. But, he had found solace in Luke. But the government demanded his grandson for the war effort. He was as powerless as a pauper.*

He would receive two letters from Luke, but he would never touch, see, or hear his grandson again.

"Mr. Cratchit," Elsie spoke.

Timothy Cratchit looked around the great room to see Elsie standing in her "official" capacity stance.

"Dr. Strauss, to see you, sir."

"Strauss, on Christmas Eve?" Cratchit inquired.

The short, balding physician, clad in a full dress winter coat and wire spectacles stepped into the room without waiting for a formal invitation. He began to take his coat off and when he was finished he handed it to Elsie, who left the room to hang the wrap.

"Hello, Mr. Cratchit. Merry Christmas and all the blessings of the season to you and your household."

"I appreciate your sentiment, Strauss. But as you know, the walls and doors cannot wish you a "Merry Christmas". My hearth and mantle cannot bestow you the blessings of a "happy New Year", so you'll have to allow me to speak their feeling for them."

The doctor stood perplexed a moment, but soon realized Cratchit's quick wit had indulged in sarcasm.

"See my family, doctor. This house. It's all that is left of my legacy. And you'll have to forgive me if I find it to be no comfort at all."

The doctor thought a moment as the two sat down upon a luxurious antique sofa. "You know, Timothy, that the grieving process is natural. It's been only two months since you received word of Luke's death. It is natural that you wouldn't be in a mood for Christmas festivities. But it's important that you go on."

"Go on?" Cratchit scolded. "Go on, for what? You didn't hear me a moment ago. What's left is this house. Brick, mortar, sticks. It will go on fine without me."

"It is my duty as your physician when I see you engaged in self-destructive habits to point that out to you and help find the remedy. My profession is not only one of healing, but one of instruction."

"Instruction?" Cratchit latched onto the word. "Well, if it's instruction you offer, then show me how to die."

"Eighty-one years old, the body and mind of a man twenty years younger, and you talk of dying. That isn't going to happen any time soon, but it will come sooner than it needs to if you continue in this self-destructive attitude. Come to my home and join my family tomorrow. You can enter through the alley so that you won't be observed going into a German home on Christmas if you wish."

"If I had desire to walk in your front door, I would do it proudly, Dr. Strauss. You know that, sir. I have an invitation for Christmas tomorrow...."

"Good," the doctor interrupted, "Elsie, and her family, of course."

"But I have no intention of leaving this house tomorrow, unless it is a matter of divine intervention. And you just told me that the event I so desire is not likely to happen."

"Being a physician is so frustrating. I am helpless in aiding so many that are younger than you to obtain health who seek wellness, but are denied it due to years of physical neglect. And then there is you, in optimal health who wishes to die."

"It is Christmas. I've given bonuses to my servants, I've given money to war orphans and widows, and I've paid the supreme price of my grandson to the war effort. If I wish to spend a solitary Christmas, that should be my affair, now shouldn't it?"

"Your generosity has been the finest this city has ever known, Mr. Cratchit. Indeed, your love for your fellow man regardless of race or creed has been a sterling example for this often narrow-minded city to follow. But why don't you show compassion for yourself."

"Are you suggesting I commit suicide, Dr. Strauss?" Cratchit asked in a most matter of fact tone.

"Unfortunately, that is not an option that I would consider. My faith has not faltered to that point. I didn't decide to be born, at least not consciously, so it is not my decision as to when I shall die. But it doesn't mean that I cannot wish that the hour would come."

Visibly, Strauss was frustrated. "You know fully well that I am not suggesting suicide. Quite the opposite. I don't want you to die; I want you to live! Live fully, Cratchit. You have Elsie, you have me and my family, and your businesses, and brothers and sisters still living overseas, as well as nieces and nephews."

"Whom I will never see again, due to this damned old war."

"The war won't last forever, Mr. Cratchit."

"Won't it?" asked Timothy. He thought of Luke; for him, it had lasted forever. Therefore, Cratchit could see no reason why it would ever end.

The doctor assured him, "Seasons pass and change. We all have little time, some more than others. Nothing lasts forever, not even a war."

Timothy Cratchit was not convinced.

## Stave Two- Ebeneezer Scrooge

Being Christmas Eve, the employees of Timothy Cratchit's household promptly left at 6 PM to be with their respective families. Elsie, however, stayed behind to reiterate her greeting of the season, but found Cratchit resolute in his determination to keep a somber Christmas alone. Knowing that she was needed at home for the festivities that were to follow that evening, she did some preparation of Cratchit's morning breakfast. This would make the meal easier for the gentleman to manage in the morning, since she would be celebrating Christmas at home, and Cratchit had vowed to be alone.

"Is there anything I can do for you before I go, Mr. Cratchit?" she implored.

"No."

"Your breakfast is in the kitchen. All you have to do is serve it to yourself. It's all ready."

Cratchit looked around the parlor. His eyes fixed on a large model sailboat that was displayed on the mantel. "Do you see that model, Elsie?"

"The ship? I guess I do."

"That was for Luke. I picked it up in a shop in Baltimore shortly before his parents died. I was planning to send it to him for Christmas. But being, how his parents were killed on a boat, I could not bring myself to give him that gift. I put it away for a few years, but the little rascal found it and drug it out. I never did tell him that I bought it for him."

Elsie sighed, "Master Luke knew he could get something from you, and that was love."

"I loved him. I still love him. As much as this old heart is capable of love," the old man muttered.

"You are capable of love and worthy of it too. Please come home with me and spend Christmas Eve with us," the kind woman pleaded.

The elderly gentleman shook his head and looked away.

"Merry Christmas, Mr. Cratchit. God bless you, Mr. Cratchit," Elsie affirmed as she gathered her things and made her way out of the house to be with her family that awaited her this Christmas Eve.

As she left, pain tore in Cratchit's heart. Anger? Perhaps, but when pain is as persistent as it was for Cratchit, the definition of the torment is futile. He looked out the window and could see a few flickering candles and a distant Christmas tree at a neighboring house not far from his estate. He had always loved the season, but this year there was only the solitary tree in the parlor that had been lit only once; this was the only Yuletide adornment. There was nothing for him to celebrate this year.

His mind remained on Luke and the pain that the loss had caused him. The arrival of the boy in his life and heart had been a bittersweet affair since it came at the loss of his only son, but oh the exultation and delight that Luke had brought to his life. Many credited Cratchit's longevity with his having a reason to truly enjoy living. But now, Cratchit could not see why his life should go on when Luke's had ended.

As much as Cratchit was wishing his own death imminent at this moment, such had not been the case during the Christmas of 1909. Timothy Cratchit had held a grand Christmas gala on December 23 for all his employees of his house and business. To fully accommodate all the employees and their large families, he had chosen to hold the affair in the large hall that adjoined his manor home. The party had been a greater celebration than most of the working class Cincinnatians had ever known. Not wanting to burden his employees with the clean up, Cratchit sent them all on their merry way. Elsie took twelve year old Luke to main house against the youth's wishes. The young man expressly stated his desire to remain with his grandfather, but the matronly Elsie would have none of that.

Once alone, Timothy Cratchit prepared to extinguish a large burning candle at the top of the huge Christmas tree that embellished the room. Standing on a make shift ladder,

Cratchit fell head long into the mammoth pine. His forehead impacted squarely with the stone floor, rendering him instantly unconscious. As the tree fell, the still burning candle came in contact with a linen tablecloth that instantly ignited in a flame. Indeed the inanimate gentleman would have perished had Luke not sneaked away from Elsie's watchful eye to rejoin his grandfather. Upon entering the hall, the young man dragged his grandfather out of the fire's path and summoned help. It goes without saying the bond the two had was bonded even more securely at that point, with Cratchit often referring to young Luke as the hero.

He had wanted to live then; now, he did not.

He walked to where the message lay and picked it up. He read the words to himself: "Luke Jacob Cratchit, US Army Recruit 2930-745-836, was killed 10-30-17 during air maneuvers in preparation for battle......" The old man cried as if he were reading the words for the first time. Luke was gone. Luke was gone for good.

Presently, he heard the building sound of choral voices that were increasing. Peering into the darkness from his window, he could see figures of children approaching with adults in the role of supervisor tailing behind. As the carolers neared Cratchit's door, he found himself involuntarily wishing them gone. But this was not to be.

Stopping directly in front of Cratchit's entry door, they stopped walking while continuing to sing, "God Rest Ye Merry Gentlemen". Becoming increasingly obvious to Cratchit that they were seeking his recognition, he managed good-naturedly to gather some lose fruit, mostly apples and oranges, open his doors and treat the carolers. They thanked him and he even managed a pleasant smile. As he closed the door, he found himself besieged with a flood of season's greetings and a barrage of "Merry Christmas" resonating as the chorus continued on with another carol.

His spirit grew weak, and he wished to curse or do something by way of defiance to the season. Yes, now it was anger and it had burst violently within his soul.

"Balderdash!" he shrieked aloud. "It's Christmas, but what good is it? The world's at war; my grandson is dead! It's all unfair!"

He looked around the room as if trying to find something to comfort him, but he realized that his violent soliloquy did aid his general feeling of well-being, so he endeavored to continue in some way, although the proper words seemed to escape him.

Finally, falling back to the slang of his childhood, he found the proper term. "It's humbug! That's what it is!" Now, he shouted quite loudly, "Humbug!"

For a moment, silence pervaded, but then he heard a non-descript tapping at the door. It was the same door from behind which stood the carolers only moments earlier. Had they returned?

But no, he had seen them turn to the next street, and he heard no singing.

The tapping was more definite when it came the second time, and Timothy chuckled at the resemblance of his plight to the famous narrative poem of Edgar Allan Poe.

Muttering a line from the poem, "Ah, distinctly I remember, it was in that bleak December...," Cratchit made his way to the door and opened it.

Standing in the door way was a man, perhaps the same age as Cratchit dressed in an English style of half a century ago, with a waistcoat, bright red vest, and a shining black top hat. Still, the item that made him look most peculiar was the torch like device he carried as if on some mission from long ago. Instantly the man spoke, "Merry Christmas, Timothy. You're looking quite well this Christmas Eve."

Not waiting for an invitation, the stranger made his way into the parlor, erected his torch (with its flame still constant) near the hearth, and began taking off his wraps.

Cratchit stood visibly perplexed. "Sir, is there something I can help you with? I return the greetings of the season, but I'm quite sure I don't know you," Cratchit said without any conviction in his voice. (He did know this man, but he *knew* that his being here on this night was impossible.)

Turning to Cratchit, the stranger spoke in the most good-natured of terms, as one greets a loved one after a long absence. "Tim, how have you been?" The stranger warmly took the hand of his reluctant host who resisted this as well.

"Sir, if it's hospitality you seek, you're welcome to warm yourself by the fire, but I don't know you." Cratchit was shaking as the words fell from his lips.

"Tim, don't be afraid. It's me, Uncle Ebeneezer. Mr. Scrooge. Remember?"

Tim looked shocked, then regained composure. "That's impossible, and it's not funny! Now, I'll be pleased to overlook this incident if you will take your form from off my door." With a gesture of his hand, he brushed the visitor away.

"Poe? Hmm, Tim? That's good - you always were fond of literature. Good to hear you quoting poetry," the man said. He stroked his chin, squinted his eyes and recited: " 'Take thy beak from out my heart and take thy form from off my door-Quoth the raven, "Nevermore." ' "

"What are you doing here?" Cratchit demanded of the stranger.

"Well first of all," the stranger began, "I'm going to light that Christmas tree. It's Christmas Eve, my boy."

Cratchit winced at being called "boy" for the first time in

more than sixty years.

"Who are you?"

"I told you. I'm Mr. Ebeneezer Scrooge. And I come in honor of the season that was my reclamation!"

"Mr. Scrooge? Impossible, Mr. Scrooge died in 1867."

The stranger replied, as if picking up where Cratchit left off, "Leaving fifty percent of his business to his nephew, Fred Holloway, and fifty percent to his faithful employee of thirty years, Mr. Bob Cratchit, your father."

"Yes, that's true. But, how can this be? You can't be the same Ebeneezer Scrooge that's been buried in London some fifty years!"

"This earth upon which you live now, Timothy Cratchit, is but a shadow of the workings of this world. There are many miracles of which you know nothing of, but they are real, Tim, as real as anything that may be happening on this little planet. Even more real, for many things that go on here are but a façade-they have no reality in and of themselves. They are simply necessary to complete the play so to speak. Bill Shakespeare was right-'all the world's a stage'."

Timothy Cratchit sat down and held his head in his hands. "No, this - this can't be. This is senseless."

Old Scrooge laughed. "You don't mean to say, my good boy, that just because you don't understand something means that it cannot be, do you?"

Cratchit thought for a moment and, sure enough, he was starting to believe what his mind did not want to accept. He *was* in the presence of Ebeneezer Scrooge, the gentleman who had saved his life from a deadly childhood disease- the man who had rescued his family from poverty. Most enigmatic, he appeared to be talking to a man who was present in the flesh (Scrooge was far more corpulent than ethereal), and whose funeral he had attended on another continent some fifty years earlier. Even if by some unexplained miracle Old Scrooge were still alive, he would have to be at least 130 years old!

Pointing to the hearth where rested his visitor's torch, Cratchit commented, "That's a peculiar lighting apparatus. May I intrude upon you to ask its purpose?"

"I am a way shower!" Scrooge announced.

"The Way shower?" Cratchit asked.

"No, I said that I am *a* way shower. There are many of us, you know," Scrooge said as if the correction were an obvious one. "Perhaps the best one of all is the reason for the season, as some say."

As if he finally realized what was going on, Timothy Cratchit spoke softly, "Uncle Ebeneezer, you've come to take me home, correct? I wished to die, and that's why you're here. Of course! This is death, isn't it?"

Scrooge, for the first time since his arrival, spoke sternly,

" This is not death, Timothy! This is life! And it's a life that you have been given abundantly." Turning to the Christmas tree again, he continued, "And it's Christmas. Perhaps the only time left when men and women seem by one accord……….."

" 'By one accord to open their shut up hearts'" Cratchit continued the lines, " 'A kind, charitable forgiving time.' Yes, the words of your nephew, Fred. My father quoted them often. But if this isn't death, how are you here?"

Ignoring the question for the moment, Scrooge replied, "Those words are why I am here, Timothy. Those words and the deeds behind them are why I am here. Christmas is perhaps the grandest of all Earth's celebrations. But you're not keeping Christmas in your home! And you're not keeping it in your heart."

Timothy spoke slowly, "I have kept Christmas, in past years, but my heart is weary. I'm tired. I wish to…" He appeared ashamed of his words. "I wish to die."

"And I wish for you to live, Timothy. You don't want to die."

"I do," Cratchit protested. "Luke is dead; he was my reason for living and that reason is now void."

Scrooge smiled and spoke, "Luke doesn't want you to die."

Timothy looked up, suddenly very interested in what

Ebeneezer Scrooge was stating. "Do you know Luke?"

Scrooge nodded affirmatively, "I do."

"How, how is he? Can I see him?" implored the elderly man.

"You're willing to listen to me, I see now"

"I am. I will listen to what you have to say." Poor old Cratchit could hardly contain his excitement.

"I know that you want to hear about Luke, and I promise that I will not disappoint you in that matter. But we have tonight, Christmas Eve, for you to attend to some affairs. In closing Christmas out of your heart, you are contributing to this Great War!"

Cratchit was offended. "Me? Contributing to the war? Outrageous!"

"No," Scrooge said. "It's not outrageous at all. In closing yourself up to your own most sacred of holidays, you miss its real meaning and cannot grasp its deeper meaning of love and unity of the entire human race."

"Explain it to me, then. No, I do not conceive the meaning of this at all, "Cratchit said.

"Now, where to begin?" Scrooge asked thoughtfully. "In terms that you can presently comprehend, I suppose I should go back to London, 1843."

"London, 1843; I would have been seven years old," Cratchit observed.

"Yes, the youngest son of my clerk, Bob Cratchit. A man who served me well in more ways than he ever knew," Scrooge muttered, half aloud and half to himself.

"And you, Uncle Ebeneezer, served us well. Was that the year that you surprised us with a turkey that was bigger than I was at the time?" Timothy Cratchit asked.

Scrooge laughed heartily. "Yes, yes it was. You were but a little boy - Tiny Tim, you were called. But do you remember the puzzlement that your parents experienced trying to figure out from where that huge fowl had originated?"

"Because you had sent it anonymous," Cratchit interjected.

"Indeed, I did," Scrooge conceded, " but there was more to it than that. I had not been a kind man."

"Mr. Scrooge, please, you were the kindest man in all of London. It was a well known fact throughout England that if any man knew how to keep Christmas, it was you," Timothy explained. "No doubt, that's why you are here now, but as you know, I have little reason to make merry this Christmas. Forgive me, Uncle Ebeneezer."

The specter Scrooge sighed. "There is nothing to forgive, Timothy. We only need to correct our errors, as I did mine. Yes, I often forget that you were too young to remember the Ebeneezer Scrooge that I had been for the first sixty-two years of my life. To my memory's benefit, it was kind of your father not to remind you."

Puzzled, Timothy Cratchit stated, "I do not understand."

As if gaining a bit of insight, Scrooge began, "You *do* know the name Jacob Marley."

"Yes, your partner; it was your request to have one of my son's named after him. But I named my *only* son after you and father, Ebeneezer Robert Cratchit. So naturally, I was thrilled when he and his wife agreed to give the middle name "Jacob" to Luke, their only son as fate would have it.

"Yes, on behalf of myself *and* Jacob Marley, I thank you for that. Without Jacob Marley, I don't know what have become of you *or* me. Or perhaps it would be more correct to say that *I do know how we would have ended up.*"

Cratchit was very interested. "Tell me more, Uncle Ebeneezer."

"I shall, Timothy, indeed I shall-just the same as Old Marley showed me, but I will try to be a bit more gentle than he. Not to say that I didn't need a bold awakening. And you need it too, Tim, albeit of a different nature. You have tasted the milk of human kindness and freely given it back, a trait that I lacked prior to my dealings with a spectral Marley and three spirits of Christmas."

Certainly, Cratchit seemed perplexed. "I am at loss, and most confused, Ebeneezer Scrooge. Mr. Marley, three spirits, Christmas Eve, 1843- yes, I recall your story that you told, and I have derived much good from it. But what has this to do with me now? What brings you here?"

Childless on earth, Scrooge never looked more paternal. "It will be explained, Tim. All of it-by me, and by three spirits of Christmas."

Trying to grasp the meaning of his benefactor's words, Cratchit asked, "The ones who visited you?"

Shaking his head, Scrooge answered, "No, no. Like I said, you have a different lesson to learn. I was visited by the ghosts of Christmas Past, Present, and Future as it pertained to my own life. This was necessary for my redemption, because of my hardness and bitterness."

"I have tried not to be bitter," Timothy stated in a melancholy voice.

"The only bitterness you harbor is toward yourself. But you have value, Tim! And I'm not talking about your wealth. God has given you much because of the way you use your talents and money to benefit others! No man can give up on himself, whether he's eighteen or eighty-one! I will stay with you tonight, Timothy, and we shall host three spirits."

Timothy, now visibly frightened, protested, "I am an old man. I cannot bear these ghosts."

"That is why I shall stay with you. You have nothing to

fear, but everything to gain! The first spirit will be here shortly. It is the Spirit of Christmas That Might Have Been. It's an old spirit; it never happened and it won't happen now, but we can learn from the lessons that might have been if we don't dwell on them. Tonight, we'll only visit."

"And the others?" asked Timothy Cratchit.

"There is the Spirit of Christmas in Your Heart. Those are the memories that never go away. The ones you carry with you. And finally, you will meet the Spirit of Christmas That May Still Be. You will get a rare glimpse of what the future may hold for you. You may be an old man in earth years, but there is still plenty left for you to do here. Otherwise, you'd be gone already. Are you willing to learn, Tim?"

"People usually look to me for advice. I seldom seek it anymore. But this interchange between you and me baffles me, yet intrigues like nothing I've ever seen."

"Then you'll welcome the Spirits of Christmas into your home tonight?" asked Scrooge.

"Agreed," smiled Cratchit.

"Excellent," replied Scrooge, "then, help me light these candles, and make up the room. Our Christmas guests will arrive soon."

"Will I meet Mr. Marley?" Cratchit asked.

"No," Scrooge stated, "Jacob's very busy tonight-still

working on some of the more primitive cases such as a I was in '43. Now, we have work to do in getting ready for Christmas."

If a stranger were to gaze through a window into the room, he would not be able to tell that the two elderly gentlemen were anything but old friends. As the two, one physical and one spectral, lit the many candles in the room and on the Christmas tree, a spirit of the season pervaded the air of Cratchit's manor for the first time that year, 1917.

## Stave Three- The Christmases That Might Have Been

Whether its 1843 Victorian England or 1917 Cincinnati, Ohio, a magical quality pervades the atmosphere beginning around the 9 PM hour on Christmas Eve and remains prevalent into the pre-dawn and dawn hours of Christmas morning. A glimmer of the enchantment can be felt at times preceding and proceeding this interval, but positively nothing surpasses this marvelous interim. Even in trenches of warfare, miraculous tales of cease fire and a spirit of goodwill toward all men often flow in men's hearts who are otherwise intent on killing each other. Though the wonders vary by degree, Christmas breaks boundaries of many kinds.

It was at the beginning of the nine o'clock hour when Timothy Cratchit and the supernatural visitor in the person of Mr. Ebeneezer Scrooge finished lighting the Christmas tree. The elderly gentlemen sat and had coffee and tea. (Scrooge, being the eternal Englishman had tea, while the Americanized Cratchit had coffee.)

"You're really here, aren't you, Ebeneezer Scrooge?" asked Tim Cratchit as Scrooge took a drink of tea. "I mean, you're drinking real tea, so you must really be here."

"As clever and as observant as your father. Of course, back when I thought only of physical productivity, his mind was the sole reason for which I hired him. But hiring your father is one of the few things from those early days that I do not regret. He was a powerful asset to me in many ways, Tim. Ways that, like I said earlier, he knew nothing of."

"Uncle Ebeneezer, you keep speaking of those early days. Have you really that many regrets, sir?"

Scrooge answered quickly, "Oh, yes, I could have, 'tis true, but I don't dwell on it. I only revisit from time to time."

Cratchit seemed confused. "But whatever for?"

"Only," Scrooge began, "for the good I can derive from it. And sometimes on earth, it is generative to look to our past and see what might have been, both the good and the bad, to the reflect where we are now."

The words had no more than left old Scrooge's lips when a mist inaugurated the room. At first, all that was visible was a rainbow of colors in a vapor that seemed to illuminate the Christmas tree to a greater intensity. In front of where Cratchit and Scrooge sat, a mystical fog descended from the vault of the ceiling that became more distinct with a passing moment, but still not so definite that one might distinguish all the features of the being.

While peering at the vaporous entity, Cratchit commented, "I am not seeing it well. Who or what is it?"

A distinct authoritarian voice of a woman answered, "I am the Ghost of Christmas that might have Been."

Rising, Scrooge assumed the role of welcoming agent. "Merry Christmas, Spirit! We have been eagerly awaiting your arrival."

Cratchit glanced at Scrooge and winced a little when Scrooge uttered the word, "eagerly".

The ghost, still speaking frankly, stated, "Remember, Ebeneezer Scrooge, that my visits are not always pleasant for I bring the details of what might have been had interceding circumstances not occurred."

"Yes Spirit, I, more than most, am painfully aware of how compelling a visit from the spirits of Christmas may be, but we have the pleasure of being in the company of Timothy Cratchit, a gentleman and one of the greatest philanthropists on two continents."

The Ghost interjected, "You and I are both aware of the good that Mr. Cratchit has done on this earth for others, but he has not fully understood love."

Cratchit, silent to this point, felt it necessary to speak, "I *do* know how to love-I have love for *all* my fellow man, but please understand that I feel that I am presently deprived of all the great loves of my life. Surely, you understand the loss of love, Sprit, don't you?"

As if ignoring Cratchit's question, the Ghost of Christmas That Might Have Been addressed Cratchit in a general way. "For you, Timothy Cratchit, my presence will not be painful, but it will be an emotional journey."

"I've watched my parents die, suffered the loss of my son and grandson, and watched all that I've valued be ripped apart by a war. I see how nothing you could tell me would bring a further emotional response from me."

Scrooge, the obvious voice of experience, spoke softly to Cratchit, "I won't leave you, my boy. We'll visit what might have been together."

The vapor spirit led them to the door. "Come, we have many years to cover."

"Years?" Cratchit thought aloud. He concluded this to be a peculiar way of measuring distance. "Just where are we going?" the old man inquired.

Scrooge, headed for the door, picked up his torch, but left his overcoat behind, commenting that they would not need protection from the cold on this journey.

Cratchit, having regained some of his determination that he had earlier surrendered to Scrooge, commented, "If I am to die, I have no intention of it being by the grips of pneumonia."

However, when Scrooge opened the door of the parlor, the spirit led them *not* into the windy Cincinnati night where Cratchit had earlier received Christmas carolers, but into a time and place that Scrooge and Cratchit knew well. It was now daylight and the air felt different. It smelled different. Openness and a more distinct clatter of horses reigned throughout the city. The buildings no longer towered as high, but were far more plentiful. Cratchit was in the same London, England that he had known as a seven-year-old lad in 1843.

Instantly, Cratchit turned to inspect the door from which he had exited. It in no way resembled the front door of Cratchit manor, but instead belonged to an earlier period and served a much more conservative purpose. Although it had been many years, he distinctly remembered this as a door he stood outside of many times in his earliest years in life waiting for his father. As if to reassure himself, he looked up to see the sign above the entry of the counting house. Looking weathered, though no more than it had in his childhood, it read clearly in gothic English-styled lettering: *Scrooge and Marley.*

Aghast, Timothy Cratchit cried, "We're back in London. At your counting house! Your *old* counting house."

Scrooge managed only a slight smile and nodded. (Shortly after his interludes with the Spirits of Christmas Past,

Present, and Future, Scrooge had abandoned this dismal counting house for a more respectable looking office, where he gave Robert Cratchit a fine working environment and three assistants. Only seven, Tiny Tim had only fragmented memories of Scrooge's former self and knew only that he had spent very little time *inside* the old counting house, but had many fond recollections of the new office. Eventually, Cratchit served an apprenticeship there and had later taken over the office himself before moving the operation to America shortly after the death of his parents in 1876.)

"Does the date December 26, 1843, mean anything to you, Timothy Robert Cratchit?" the shade of a spirit asked.

Cratchit pondered a moment. "Well, no, except that it was the day after perhaps one of my earliest and fondest memories of Christmas-thanks to Ebeneezer Scrooge, here."

Scrooge smiled only faintly.

"You remember what happened on the previous day. But let us go inside and see a remnant of the Christmas that might have been," instructed the spirit.

Tim Cratchit said aloud as if thinking, "This really is London. I've crossed an ocean by stepping out of my door in Cincinnati and onto a London street! And it's not 1917- it's 1843."

Scrooge fully understood Cratchit's confusion. "Amazing, from your perspective, I know. But it's all perfectly natural in the non-physical world."

"But I am of the physical world," Cratchit affirmed.

"Partially, yes-you are having a physical experience these past eighty years or so. But you are a spiritual being. Period. The physical lasts only so long then you move on."

The Spirit of Christmas That Might Have Been stated frankly, "We do have work to accomplish. There is no need to procrastinate."

"Let's go," said Scrooge to Cratchit, "these spirits can get a bit testy at times!"

Together, the spirit, Scrooge and Cratchit made their way into the tiny office door.

Although it must have been cold outside, Tim did not seem to notice any external chill until he stepped into this den of dismal, musty ledgers. A smell of coal ashes existed in the room, but without any evidence of their warmth.

Approaching from the rear of the room, Cratchit caught the back view of a tattered man, wrapped in a worn white comforter and wearing a bedraggled brown overcoat. Cratchit fixed his gaze upon the man. "Father!" he pronounced in an excited whisper.

Fixing himself so that he could view the weary man's face, Cratchit did not even notice the troubles that were evident on the man's countenance. Timothy could see that his father was talking to Ebeneezer Scrooge, who looked hardened and angry. Dressed in a non-descript conservative black suit, Scrooge sat in sharp contrast to the Ebeneezer Scrooge who had accompanied him here. Although the two Scrooges appeared of a near equal age, the demeanor and dress of the two stood worlds apart- the kindly Scrooge aglow and sharply dressed displaying the splendor of the season while the one speaking to his father was harsh, cruel, and stern. Timothy listened to the conversation his father was having with Scrooge.

"It shall not be repeated, Mr. Scrooge. I was making rather merry yesterday," Tim heard his father explain.

"Making rather merry," mocked Scrooge. "I am a man of business. Business knows no merry making. And therefore, neither can I. Your services are no longer needed, Cratchit. I paid you fifteen shillings on the twenty-fourth of December, so our ties are finished. And since I've had to dismiss you as a punitive measure, there will be no severance compensation."

"But Mr. Scrooge, please, my family is dependent on this job. Cut my wages, sir and I'll work longer hours, but I pray you do not dismiss me."

Scrooge was resolute. "I do not tolerate begging on the street, and I certainly won't put up with it in my office. You are dismissed; it's time for you to be gone, Cratchit. See yourself out now."

Robert Cratchit turned dejectedly, gathered a meager supply of copying goods from his desk and turned to leave.

"Father!" cried Timothy.

"He can't hear you, Tim." Scrooge explained.

Angrily, Timothy demanded, "Why did you do that? He was very loyal to you."

At this, the spirit interceded, "This is what might have been, Timothy. It did not happen. But it might have been, had Mr. Scrooge not have had a change of heart. This might have been, but it was not due to the actions of Mr. Scrooge."

"I understand, Spirit. Perhaps I have not been as grateful as I should have been. Forgive me, Mr. Scrooge, Uncle Ebeneezer," Cratchit cried.

"You do *not* understand, Tim," Scrooge answered. "You're gratitude has never been in question. Just observe, Tim. The meaning will become clear later tonight. For now, just observe, and (pointing to the miser Scrooge at the desk) let's leave this unhappy soul. If we pay him no mind, we deny him the power to hurt others. This principle alone is sufficient lesson from this encounter."

"It's time to move on," uttered the spirit, and the party stepped onto the London street proceeding to a destination unknown to Cratchit. As they moved past the counting house window, Cratchit noticed the fading of the miser Scrooge, until he was no more visible-less visible perhaps- than the Spirit of Christmas That Might Have Been.

They had gone only a few paces when Cratchit asked, "Now, where are we going?"

Scrooge smiled a genuine smile this time. "Would like to see your family, Timothy? And yourself as you were in 1843?"

"Is that possible?" asked Cratchit, knowing the answer even before he spoke the words given the unworldly occurrences of this night that had already transpired.

The spirit spoke in its detached manner to both of them. "It is necessary that you do this, Timothy Cratchit, but remember that the events that transpire will not be as you remember them. They are only what might have been."

Scrooge shook his head in puzzled bewilderment and looked upward, stating both to Cratchit and to the sky simultaneously, "Spirits? Go figure them out, will you? Such temperamental beings."

The party of three walked on for several city blocks, watching the plentiful industrial buildings dwindle into smaller shanties, the dwellings of the working class poor.

At last, they ventured to the place that Cratchit remembered as the home of his early childhood.

The spirit glanced at Scrooge, who raised his torch and the three were instantly transported inside.

To say that the quarters were compact would have been a gross understatement. Though it had never been so in Timothy Cratchit's mind, the house was cramped, nearly requiring one to have the talents of a contortionist to maneuver his way through the people and the simple furnishings.

Present were two of Tim's sisters, and Tim himself. The older Cratchits, including Tim's brother Peter, were out earning very meager wages to help support the family. Over in the corner, away from the children in the food preparation area (one could hardly call it a kitchen), sat Tim reading his school primer, a crutch resting near his chair.

Robert Cratchit sat on a stool near the fire, his face buried in his hands. Mrs. Cratchit was behind him with a trembling hand on his shoulder.

The twentieth century Timothy Cratchit took in the moment with a storm of conflicting emotions. On one hand he experienced the utter thrill of being in the same room as his parents for the first time in many years, but he was pained deeply to see them in such misery. Almost without realizing that he was doing so, he shouted, "What is troubling them so!" Then almost instantly, he realized what had happened, and worse still, he knew what it meant to them. In 1843 England, debtors with no means of paying their debts would be sent to prison and the debtor's family would at best be sent to the parish poor house. At worst, they could be separated forever or starve to death. For a crippled child like Tiny Tim Cratchit, death was a certainty.

"Spirit," cried Cratchit, "I wish to see no more."

"It is only what might have been," replied the Spirit.

"And," added Ebeneezer Scrooge, " only necessary for a sake of reference."

Cratchit did not accept this explanation, "I can not see how reference to such a wretched thing as this could ever be of any value."

"Such is the case," explained Scrooge, "of many things on this earth. They are seemingly cruel, and in fact many times are, but their value does not become clear for sometimes many earth years, and sometimes not even until we depart this planet." On somewhat of a lighter note, he added, "Fortunately for you, the reason for these things will become clear by the time the last spirit leaves here tonight."

Cratchit now remembered that Scrooge had spoken of three spirits and, being that he did not like at all what he was seeing from the first ghost, did not look forward to seeing the other two at all.

After a moment, Timothy asked Scrooge and the Spirit, "Tell me, is all that might have been bad? Are you telling me that life is as good as it possibly can be and that there is no need to try to improve?"

Scrooge spoke to the Ghost, "Oh, Spirit, I can see that the other spirits will definitely need to visit. I can see that he still does not quite yet get the picture."

Timothy, who had become more accustomed to his unusual supernatural visits mustered the courage to ask, "Spirit, tell me, why don't you fully materialize. I mean, after all, you're dreadfully hard to follow given the sparse quality of your being."

In the same unemotional tone that the Spirit had maintained throughout the night, she uttered, "I am as full in quality as I can be. I can always be seen through because I never was. You need only look through and beyond me to see what really is, and not what might have been."

Scrooge took Timothy's arm, " Timothy, my boy, this would have been the end of the line for you *and* me. Jacob Marley taught me that and I am eternally thankful to him. Because of his intervention, this Christmas scenario that might have been can never be a reality. Come Tim, let's leave you with a more pleasant memory of what might have been."

With a gentle lift of his torch, Ebeneezer Scrooge, Timothy Cratchit, and the Ghost of Christmas that Might Have Been were transported to an elegant London townhouse with a parlor that reminded Tim instantly of the period shortly after the turn of the century. Looking around the premises, Timothy Cratchit realized that he had been in this townhouse at one point in his life, but not during the festive Christmas occasion that was currently in progress. At once, he recognized Catherine Cratchit, the wife of Ebeneezer Cratchit, Timothy's only son and Luke's father. The pretty petite features of the proper British lady matched the décor of the townhouse: elegance and style abounded in the house and the spirit of Christmas permeated the air.

As the lady summoned her maid to help her place the last of the gifts under the sprawling Christmas tree, Ebeneezer Cratchit sneaked up behind his wife, kissed her on the cheek wishing her "Merry Christmas".

"He's coming down now. I heard him getting up," announced Ebeneezer Cratchit to his wife.

Enid, the maid, squealed with delight and took her place behind the parents as they awaited the young boy's arrival. The parents could hear the padded stocking feet striking the hardwood floor. Although he was twelve now, the boy still grew eager for Christmas morning just as he had in past years. It also seemed true that the parents were still eager for him to remain a child, at least on this day.

The look on the faces of Ebeneezer and Catherine Cratchit harmonized with the glow of Timothy Cratchit as they watched twelve-year-old Luke bound into the room. As the young boy's eyes took in the enormity of the festive trimmings and gifts, his parents and the doting housemaid were reveling in pride and sharing in the child's joy. A love transcended the merriment of any material quality of happiness that was present in the atmosphere.

Timothy Cratchit glanced at the still hazy Spirit and Ebeneezer Scrooge and stated emphatically, "Thank you, Spirit. Thank you, Uncle Ebeneezer for this moment."

Scrooge did not smile. "Tim, watch carefully, at what might have been."

Doing as he was instructed, he watched the boy open many gifts until he finally came to a large package that his father helped him to bring to the forefront. "Now this," said Ebeneezer Cratchit, "is a very special gift that I picked up from the port only a few weeks ago. It's from the United States of America. From your grandfather, Luke."

"May I open it now, Father?" Luke asked.

"Of course, you may," smiled Catherine Cratchit.

Tearing at the paper, Tim looked on to see what he had (or in this case, might have) given his grandson. Eagerly seeking the contents, the boy hurriedly stripped the layer of wrapping paper and lifted the lid of the box, revealing an elegant model of a ship.

The content of this box was not foreign to Timothy Cratchit. He knew it very well as the gift that he had picked up in Baltimore the spring before Luke's parents died: it was the gift he had *not* given to Luke on Christmas, 1909.

Perplexed, Timothy looked at Scrooge and the Spirit. "Why?" he asked. "What possible reason could you have in showing me this. Ebeneezer and Catherine are alive, and I would certainly have welcomed that, but I certainly could never have prevented their death! What is the meaning of this?"

Scrooge patted Timothy on the shoulder. "It will all become clearer to you as the night moves on."

"So you say," said Cratchit. "So you say."

Cratchit had no more than spoken these words when a rapping at the door interrupted the Christmas that might have been in 1909. Enid dutifully dismissed herself from the celebration to answer the call. While she was out, Luke chatted joyfully about his desire to visit his grandfather in the United States. His parents happily commented that they were looking into the possibility of a trip to America in the coming year.

Moments later, Enid arrived at the doorway. A worried look fixed upon her face as she spoke. "A gentleman is here to see you, Mr. Cratchit. He says that is quite urgent."

"A business caller on Christmas morning?" asked Catherine, throwing a puzzled glance at her husband who responded in kind.

"I'm sure that I know not what this is about," answered Ebeneezer Cratchit as he made his way out of the parlor.

Catherine busied Luke with a gift as she looked uneasily to the doorway from which her husband left.

Timothy Cratchit looked at Scrooge and the Spirit. "What's going on? I remember hearing nothing of any of this!" Catching himself, he realized that this was only what might have been. "Well, what the devil's going on?"

At this point, Enid rushed into the room in an obvious hurry. "I'll entertain Master Luke. Why don't you go join your husband."

"I don't need to be entertained," Luke protested. "Where's father?"

"Enid?" asked Catherine, "What's wrong?"

The nervous housekeeper did not have to answer this question for as she stammered for the right word, Ebeneezer rejoined the group. His face was sullen and forlorn.

"Eb, what is it?" implored his wife.

"A message from the United States," Ebeneezer Cratchit began.

"A message from Grandfather!" added Luke triumphantly.

The father placed his hand on the boy's head. "The message is about your grandfather, Luke. I don't suppose anything will make this any easier. Your grandfather died in a fire in Cincinnati two days ago."

"A fire!" exclaimed Catherine.

"It seems that Father had just completed his annual Christmas celebration for his employees. He always loved that so, and he was thought to be extinguishing some candles on a Christmas tree when apparently he slipped and fell."

"Oh, Ebeneezer, how dreadful!" Catherine exclaimed.

"Grandfather's dead?" asked a disbelieving Luke. "But he sent me this ship and he says he'll see me soon."

As the scene played itself out, Timothy Cratchit looked directly at his spectral benefactors. "What purpose could you have in showing me this? Are you saying that if my son and daughter-in-law had lived, then I would have died?"

"Yes," answered Scrooge.

"So what of it?" demanded Cratchit angrily. "Don't you know how many times I've asked Heaven why they were taken and *not* me? Don't you realize that I would have welcomed that exchange? I would willingly die this moment if any one of them could live, and yet, you haunt me with this ludicrousness!"

"We'll leave this place, *forever,*" answered the Spirit.

"No, wait!" Cratchit protested.

But it was too late. Instantly the Spirit had transported Timothy Cratchit and Ebeneezer Scrooge across the Atlantic and back to America. However, the locality was unknown to Cratchit. Although humid and heavy, the air felt warmer than that of Cincinnati or London in December.

The land on which they stood was not a city or even much of a town. In an open field not more than sixty yards wide, they perched next to railroad tracks, which on the north side held a quaint charming village that Cratchit recognized through his travels as the Southern United States. By contrast, to the south stood gray board structures with rusted tin roofs that may have gone unnoticed had they not been so plentiful. The simple shacks were so great in number that it appeared that the entire south section of town were a massive dingy cluster of gray huddled with matching smoke from the shanty chimneys.

"Which way are we going?" asked Timothy Cratchit.

"The lifestyles of one community is not foreign to you, though the attitudes may be," answered the spirit. "Still, it would be of little benefit for you to visit this area."

Cratchit responded, "I do not understand."

At this point, Scrooge interceded. "Timothy, we are in Mississippi. The time is Christmas, 1912. If our previous visitation were true, this *might have been* Christmas for your family in 1912."

"If I had died December 23, 1909, why would Ebeneezer move Catherine and Luke to Mississippi. If they were coming to America, they would have come to Cincinnati!" Timothy asserted.

"True, true," Scrooge assured him, " but that would not have happened either. Catherine would never leave her parents in London, and Ebeneezer would never ask her to. I'm not talking about Ebeneezer and Luke. I'm talking about your other family. I am speaking of Elsie."

"Elsie? Elsie's here?" Cratchit asked, pointing to the north side of the tracks.

"No," assured Ebeneezer Scrooge. "She's over there." Scrooge pointed to the shanties of the black workers. The housing projects of the blacks of Mississippi, 1912, barely surpassed the housing of slaves a half century earlier, and were in fact no better than the sharecropper shacks of the post-Civil War.

"Shall we go?" asked the spirit.

Cratchit had a fixed look upon his face. Without saying a word, he walked the width of the field with Scrooge and the spirit. Upon reaching the row of houses, Cratchit asked, "Where is she? Where is Elsie and what is she doing here?"

"She's with her mother-in-law. After your death, she and Benjamin could not make it in Cincinnati on the meager wages that Ben made. Elsie couldn't find work. After a time, the money you left her was exhausted as the bulk of your estate went to Ebeneezer. Elsie and Ben could no longer survive in Cincinnati so they had to move their family down here in order to make ends meet. She works scrubbing the floors and doing the linens for the whites of the community. Coming back to the South has been an adjustment, but she and Ben have learned their place."

"Their place?" asked Cratchit. "Their good hard working human beings. Their place is anywhere they want it to be."

Scrooge nodded, "Certainly, that's what their place is, but it's not what it might have been."

Without walking, the spirit transported the party into one of the shacks where he saw an elderly black woman, frail and thin, sitting next to a fire. Looking ragged and burdened next to her sat his beloved Elsie, her face tear-stained and aged, much more than her 1917 self. Benjamin stood above her, clearly a nervous, world-beaten man, so unlike the Benjamin that he knew in reality.

"The other children will be coming in soon, Ben. What are we to tell them about their brother? They'll know that something bad is wrong when Nathaniel doesn't show up for Christmas," Elsie stated.

The elderly woman spoke up, speaking to no one directly, "The young 'uns gotta larn thet thet's the way it is. We ain't free peoples and we never did be!"

"Mama," Benjamin began, "my children's been born and raised in Cincinnati. Now things are not perfect there, but they don't know about hatred the way it breeds down here. They still think their brother's staying with Mr. Robinson over in Mercer County attending his school. They were expecting him home for Christmas though."

Elsie stood and embraced her husband. She spoke to him softly. "The lawyer says there's *no* chance, Ben?" she asked, not wanting to believe what she knew the answer to be. "He hasn't even had a trial yet and he's been in that jail since the fourth of September."

"Elsie, chile," this ain't no Cinsnatty! This is Mississippi! You's in the south, girl. Ain't no nigger gonna git no trial til the sheriff good an ready to release the boy."

Elsie stood proud. "Mother Sarah, I know that I may not be familiar with the ways of the South, and I mean you no disrespect, but my Nathaniel is not a nigger. And neither am I, my husband, or any of my children or you either. No man, woman, or child on God's earth is anything other than one of His children. I am a child of God, like every body on both sides of these railroad tracks and both sides of the Mason Dixon Line!"

"Hear, hear!" cried Cratchit turning to his contemporaries, smiling. "Whether she's in Cincinnati or Mississippi or Timbuktu, Elsie is a proud woman." Turning to Elsie, he said, "You tell it like it is, Elsie. And I love you for it. So much for your place!" he added triumphantly.

Scrooge began to explain, "Elsie had raised her children to be proud. But as you know, in Mississippi, and throughout the South, blacks cannot attend the same schools as whites, and the only black high school for miles is over at Zebediah Robinson's school in Mercer County."

"Education of her children is very important to Elsie," Cratchit added.

Scrooge continued, " Nathaniel's a very polite boy, but he did not understand the ways of this region of the country. So one morning, when he smiled at a young lady, some trouble began."

"A jealous boyfriend?" asked Cratchit.

"No," said Scrooge, " the girl was white. Her brother and father took Nathaniel's kindness as an inappropriate gesture and nearly killed the boy, kicking and hitting him until his gushing face matched his bloody vomit that he spat from his mouth!"

"That's dreadful! Did he recover? How can I help him?" asked Cratchit.

"He's still recovering, but he's not completely well yet."

"That's dreadful." repeated Cratchit, "The cost of the hospitalization has no doubt left the family destitute!"

"There was no hospitalization. Nathaniel has done all of his recovering in jail-no hospital, no doctor."

"In jail? Whatever for? The boy was attacked!"

"Not in the eyes of the law of this land, Timothy. He's charged with making improper advances to a young lady and assaulting the father and brother."

"That's unfair! You said he was attacked! HE did nothing wrong! What can I do for them?"

The spirit spoke, "Nothing! Fortunately, however, there is nothing you need do, for these are not the things that are."

Scrooge continued, "They only might have been."

"But I want to help!" Cratchit protested.

" I'm sure you do, but my time is through, Timothy Robert Cratchit," replied the spirit.

"What?" Cratchit asked, but as he did, the trio was encircled by a great burst of white light, that temporarily blinded them and instantaneously transported them back to Cratchit's parlor in Cincinnati. When the light disappeared, Scrooge remained, but the Spirit of Christmas That Might Have Been was gone.

"Where did she go?" asked Cratchit.

"That's all from that spirit, but there will be two others," Scrooge answered. "Sit down, Tim, and let's watch the Christmas lights. It will all become clear to you soon."

But nothing was clear to Timothy Cratchit. He sat on the sofa, not sure of anything he had seen this night, and still unaware of what significance it could possibly hold.

## Stave Four- The Christmases In Your Heart

Ebeneezer Scrooge and Timothy Cratchit both sat quietly. Scrooge smiled, obviously content, while Cratchit's face gaped in bewilderment. Although the owner was puzzled, the house now stood aglow with the dazzling excitement of Christmas. Candles flickered, the hearth blazed, the tree radiated, and distantly bells from a neighborhood church could be heard.

"I do not understand," Cratchit spoke at last. "Why show me this? My family alive and dealing with my death? Elsie living like a third class citizen? Ridiculous and absurd!"

Scrooge conceded, "It is difficult to imagine Elsie in any subservient role. I suppose that because of the person she has become, it is hard to imagine her in any other capacity. But it might have been different- had certain events not transpired as they did."

Cratchit puffed his lips forward and nodded. "I suppose they might have been different." Then he added quickly, "As in fact many other things might have been. Had our ancestors not have started that abominable skin trade in the first place. Damn near was the death of America, slavery. A profligacy!"

"You spoke out against it even as a young man. I remember. Not at all a popular thing to do in England in the 1850's and 60's. Most British favored the South in the War Between the States, you know," Scrooge reminded him.

Cratchit spoke deliberately, "I've never cared much about the popular thing-only the right thing. And the way America and the world have treated its dark population is an atrocity. I've made no secret of that."

"You never did!" answered a third voice from the room. The sound came so suddenly that it startled even Scrooge who existed in this time frame as a supernatural being.

The voice belonged to a corpulent being, dressed elegantly in green velvet and ruffles of a full century ago. The male visitor, though quite portly, still maintained an air of dignity and perhaps superiority, though in a royal, rather than an arrogant manner.

Good-naturedly, Scrooge greeted him, "Well, hello, you've been expected but you still managed to take us by surprise." Turning to Tim, he said, "Timothy Cratchit, allow me to introduce you to the Ghost of Christmas In Your Heart."

"A pleasure to meet you, Timothy Cratchit, in this realm. Although an introduction hardly seems necessary as we have met many times before, just in other forms," chattered the Ghost.

"A pleasure, I'm sure," said Cratchit, although he sounded quite unsure of anything at this point. "You don't look like that last ghost!"

"Thank you," replied the spirit pleasantly, as though receiving an obvious compliment.

"The spirits," began Scrooge, "appear to mortals in ways that you can understand them. For instance, the Ghost of Christmas That Might Have Been has only a shade of reality, so therefore we can be barely see her, for she only might have existed. This ghost, on the other hand, definitely was......."

"So therefore, I am rather shapely," added the spirit humorously.

"This is too much," muttered Cratchit.

"Nonsense!" said the spirit, "We've only just begun!"

And so saying, they found themselves again out of doors and across the ocean, once again in jolly old England.

Once again it was Christmas, but the year was not 1843. It was Christmas Eve, 1855, and the trio stood outside the offices of Scrooge, Holloway, Cratchit, and Associates. Standing in stark contrast to the building that the previous ghost had shown them, the exterior of this building was adorned with greenery in honor of the festive season and was of itself a magnificent structure, quite unlike that of Scrooge and Marley. Timothy Cratchit remembered this building as the one where he had his first real office.

"Let's go inside," said Scrooge eagerly. It was obvious that Scrooge wanted to show off his good-natured self. *(And who can blame him? Every Christmas, we are reminded of his stingy, miser personality. It is not often that he gets to shine.)*

Without so much as a word, they were transported in the grand office where the three visitors found themselves in the midst of an office Christmas party of pastries, punch, and presents. Timothy saw his father looking older than when he saw them earlier, but he looked healthier and certainly happier. Fred Holloway, Scrooge's nephew tended the punch bowl, serving drinks to the employees. Ebeneezer Scrooge could be observed as an elderly man, somewhat effected by his years but still smiling and perky, much as he was as his spectral self. Tim also saw himself as a dashing young youth of nineteen. Until now, he had seen his wife and son in Luke, but he had never realized how much of himself had been apparent in his departed grandson.

Also present were the friends and business acquaintances that he had known at the time, most long dead now, as he was the youngest in the office. As Ebeneezer Scrooge made his rounds and gave office gifts to his employees, he stopped and had a seat beside nineteen year old Timothy Cratchit.

"Of course, we will exchange gifts tomorrow as we always do, but I had something that I wanted to give you now," Scrooge said to Tim. "You still plan on going to America someday."

"When you're ready to open operations over there, and after my education is complete, yes sir," answered Tim.

"Good, America needs men of your mind set. This is something I thought you'd enjoy." Scrooge handed Tim a rectangular package wrapped in plain white paper with a large green bow.

Tim accepted the package and turned it over.

"Well, why don't you open it and then examine it!" advised Scrooge cheerfully.

"All right," said Tim as he started to unwrap the gift. Carefully he lifted the contents from a box and produced a book from it. Looking at the cover, Timothy read, *"My Bondage and My Freedom* by Fredrick Douglass."

"I remember how despicable you found the slave trade when we visited America last year," Scrooge stated.

"Quite naïve, I was. I didn't know that such things still went on in the civilized world," Tim commented.

"This book is by a very talented writer named Fredrick Douglass. He was born in America into slavery. Now he's a free man, though some still put a price on his head. I think you'll find his story fascinating, though at times painful to the human spirit."

"Thank you, Uncle Ebeneezer. I shall look forward to reading it right away, perhaps tomorrow evening after Christmas festivities have tapered down."

"Good boy, Tim," said Scrooge.

The 1917 Cratchit spoke, "That book, among other things, marked a turning point in my life, you know."

The spirit stated, "The land had been carefully readied and cultivated and Mr. Scrooge merely planted a seed."

"You hated discrimination and injustice, even as a youth, Timothy," added Scrooge.

"I haven't done all I might have. Injustice still reigns supreme! Racial tension in the South. And just look at Cincinnati. My own doctor is afraid to be seen with me because of our different backgrounds. Look at the world and this senseless war its in now."

"Better to light a candle than curse the darkness," observed the spirit. "That's a Chinese proverb. It doesn't hurt you Westerners to get a little eastern culture."

"Well, I'd bargain with the devil to have stopped this war. It stole the most precious thing from me."

"This isn't the first war to have directly effected your life. Remember that you were set to move America after the winter of 1861," Scrooge reminded him. "But word of the

American Civil War broke out, and you had to stay behind. But as I recall, you didn't remain quiet."

"Perhaps I should have. You died in 1867; I am sure that I caused a large amount of trouble for you in what should have been the most peaceful years of your life," Cratchit said admittedly.

"Rubbish!" exclaimed Scrooge. "You were fighting for the just cause!"

The spirit interrupted, "Perhaps it is time we visited you during the American Civil War years. It effected you greatly although you were still in London. Let's visit, shall we say, Christmas, 1863."

A whirling in the air, a period of blackness, and a crash of broken glass put Cratchit, Scrooge and the spirit back into the office of Scrooge, Holloway, Cratchit and Associates. The office again boasted the Christmas season, but Fred Holloway looked troubled as he picked up a brick that had crashed through a windowpane of his office. Robert and Timothy Cratchit rushed into his office to see what had caused the commotion. Carefully, Fred untied a note that was attached to the brick and read aloud, "Yankee supporters are enemies of the crown and guilty of treason against England!"

"I guess someone disagreed with the talk I gave at the pub the other night," Timothy Cratchit observed. "I am sorry to have brought you into all of this with my opinions."

"Don't be ridiculous, Tim," his father reasoned. "We totally support what you said. You have ideals that are for the good of human race, which is a higher ideal than the economy of England."

Fred added, "It's like you said, Tim. Slavery is wrong. Nothing can justify it. And what it boils down to, Tim, is that it cannot go on. It has to be dealt with sooner or later or it will continue to fester. If the American South is victorious like most of England wants, there will be another war and another and another until the scourge of slavery is erased from human consciousness."

"Well, there's no need in upsetting Uncle Ebeneezer," Tim said.

From a far back doorway, the elderly Ebeneezer Scrooge appeared. "The only thing that upsets me is that after that blistering attack you made on slavery, Tim, we still have blinded folks who cannot see beyond their own pocketbooks. Notice, I call them blinded and not fools. I, unfortunately, can understand their position. I was like them once."

The old man walked over to his nephew, Fred, to attain the brick that had been thrown through the window. He examined it and the note attached to it. He chuckled and handed it Timothy. "Tim, my boy, you've taken it all wrong. Why it's a gift! Wrapped in paper."

They laughed.

"Tim, think of it as a Christmas gift from across the ocean. Not just from your black brothers and sisters, but from all of America and the rest of the world. We need to wipe slavery from the globe, permanently. They will all come to see that, not in my lifetime, I'm sure, but in yours? Perhaps, they will," Scrooge reasoned.

Handing Tim the brick, he laughed, "So, Merry Christmas, Tim."

And they all laughed.

Eighty-one year old Timothy Cratchit turned to the visitor Scrooge, who looked considerably younger than the 1863 Scrooge, and said, "You did live to see the end of the Civil War in America."

"Indeed, I did. And from beyond, I've watched you fight the good fight. For justice, for freedom," Scrooge added.

"And as you balanced your social causes with the needs of your family, you progressed, prospered, married, and had a child," the spirit added.

"Ebeneezer Cratchit was born in 1870, was he not?" asked Scrooge.

"1872. I married Elizabeth in 1870," corrected Cratchit.

"Ah, time. What is it anyway? Means nothing on this side, as you've seen tonight," Scrooge said easily.

"Your parents both died in 1875," observed the spirit.

"Within thirty-six days of each other. That was best for them; they loved each other so," commented Cratchit.

"And you took your young family to America the following year. You landed in New York and moved to Cleveland, but shortly thereafter decided to locate in Porkopolis-Cincinnati, the Gateway to the West."

So saying, the spirit transported them back in time and place to Cincinnati, 1881. It was Christmas Eve in the Cratchit home, not the present day manor estate, but a spacious home in a distinctive neighborhood. Elizabeth Cratchit marched their son, nine-year-old Ebeneezer Cratchit to his father, Timothy for chastisement.

"Well, young man," began the mother, "repeat your line for your father to hear."

Timothy began, "You are not saying naughty words on Christmas Eve, Ebeneezer?"

"The words may not be naughty by themselves, but his tone is most inappropriate and his message is deplorable," explained his mother.

"Well young man," Cratchit said to the youngster, "you've certainly upset your mother, and I feel that if you do not soon make amends, Father Christmas will not be making his rounds."

"My teacher says his name is Santa Claus," Ebeneezer said.

"Well, whomever, perhaps you better start by telling me what it was that you said," suggested Cratchit emphatically.

" I wanted to know why we were giving that box of toys to the orphan children," explained the child.

"That's not all you said, young man," reminded the mother.

"Go on, Eb. What else did you say?" asked Cratchit.

Sheepishly, the boy muttered, "I said that I did not see why you wasted your time on orphan children who did not smell good and did not appreciate anything anyway."

Looking at his wife, who managed a serious smile, Timothy drew his son to his knee, not for the sound spanking the boy expected, but for a talk with his father.

"Tell me, Ebby, what is it that you would most like to have for Christmas this year," asked Timothy. The question was most unexpected from both Elizabeth and Ebeneezer Cratchit. There was a moment's pause. "Well, go ahead, son, what do you want?"

"I want a real baseball bat like the Cincinnati Red Stockings use and a Cincinnati Red Stockings jersey and cap!" shouted the boy enthusiastically.

Timothy Cratchit laughed. "And I sincerely hope that you get it. Just as I hope that other boys and girls get what they wish for. But, Ebeneezer, Santa Claus does need his helpers, and we must all help out where we can."

"But Bradley Miller said that his father said those people who accept charity don't appreciate what we give them because they just want a hand out and they don't care enough about themselves to keep clean," Ebeneezer Cratchit explained to his father.

Cratchit thought a moment. "Perhaps Bradley Miller's father does not know what it's like to be poor. Maybe he doesn't understand that most people are doing the best they know how-the best they can. What those people need is to be educated - not to be ridiculed. Do you understand that, Eb?"

"Yes, Daddy, I do. Do you think Santa Claus will bring the Cincinnati Red Stockings bat?" the boy asked.

Timothy Cratchit laughed. "I hope that he does, Ebeneezer. Then you go over to the orphanage and show those boys over there how to play baseball with you. I think they'd like that."

"I do, too, Daddy!" young Ebeneezer exclaimed.

"You know, Ebeneezer, Uncle Ebeneezer Scrooge, the fine gentleman that I named you after, told a story about how he was once a miserly, mean person who would not help his fellow man," Tim began.

"Oh, Timothy, you're not going to tell that ridiculous fantasy of your Uncle Ebeneezer, are you?" Elizabeth asked.

"A ridiculous tale? I'm not so sure. Uncle Ebeneezer told it to be the truth, though no doubt it did have some qualities of a parable," the 1881 Cratchit said.

The 1917 Cratchit added to his contemporaries, "No doubt about it now, you were telling the truth." He paused. "I must be dead to believe all of this."

The spirit said, " No, Tim, you are very much alive, with more to learn."

"Ridiculous tale?" repeated Scrooge. "Nothing was ever more real or beneficial, I might add."

"Shh! Let's listen," demanded the spirit gently.

"What about Uncle Ebeneezer?" asked the boy.

"Well, Uncle Ebeneezer claims that he was a mean, nasty miser, and cared nothing for anybody except himself," Cratchit explained.

"That doesn't sound like what you've told me about Uncle Ebeneezer," young Ebeneezer Cratchit commented.

"No, and I must admit, I remember very little of it. But it must have been true; at least the part of him being stingy, because I do recall that when I was very young, my father worked very hard and we were very poor. Anyway, Uncle Ebeneezer Scrooge maintained to my father that three spirits of Christmas had visited him one Christmas Eve. They had shown up-one an hour- that night to tell him that the life that he had been living was of no value to anyone, and that if he did not change his ways, he would not see another Christmas."

As Cratchit told his son and wife the familiar story of Ebeneezer Scrooge, Jacob Marley and the three ghosts of Christmas, their unseen visitors spoke among themselves. "Tell me," the elderly Cratchit implored of the spirit, "were you one of the spirits of that visited Uncle Ebeneezer?"

The spirit smiled. "Not I, but you might say that we are all kindred spirits."

Ebeneezer chuckled, "Don't try to get a straight answer out of him. These spirits are devilishly difficult to get straightforward conversation."

Changing the subject, the spirit began, "You were an excellent father, Tim."

"I loved my son-still do- that helps in making one a good father," Cratchit answered modestly.

"Still," continued the Spirit, "the universe never takes a quality parent lightly, for it is the very thing that it needs to survive. When your wife took ill with dropsy and died the following year, you made do and raised Ebeneezer yourself. Love goes on, life goes on."

Ebeneezer Scrooge added, "And with that continuum, you saw your son grow into a man, marry a British girl, and take her back across the Atlantic to England to assume our European operations after Fred passed on in 1895. And then you came back to Europe for a visit during the Christmas of 1897. You wanted to spend Christmas with your family, but you had another reason for coming as well."

"Luke," Tim said. "He was born early Christmas morning, 1897 in London. The greatest Christmas I ever had! My God, he'd have been twenty years old if......." His voiced trailed off.

"Shall we see that Christmas, Timothy?" asked the spirit.

There was no wait for an answer as they found themselves outside the parlor of the home of Ebeneezer and Catherine Cratchit. A doctor came out to greet the tall, slender expectant father by announcing that mother and son were doing fine, as Ebeneezer received a pat on the back from both his father of 1897 and 1917, the latter going unnoticed.

They rushed in to see the tiny infant. The hair that would later be golden brown lay dark across the baby's crown. As the Timothy Cratchit of 1897 made his way forward to adore the child, Timothy Cratchit of the present could not resist the temptation of looking at cherished infant. He admired the baby, close at first, but the turned back toward Ebeneezer Scrooge and the Ghost of Christmas In Your Heart.

"You say that you are here for my benefit! To help me. Is that correct?" asked Cratchit.

"It is true that we have no other reason for being here," explained the spirit.

"Well," Cratchit began coldly, "I'll have to beg your pardon at the fact that I am not grateful. And I do, indeed, thank you for showing me my love ones again. But you have only convinced me of what I already know. That the people who mean the most to me are dead! That all that I am doing is waiting to die! Well, you'll have to excuse my ingratitude, but I already knew what a pitiful existence I had before you showed up. Furthermore, if you would kindly conduct me home to Cincinnati, I'd like to forget about the things that I have seen tonight. They bring me only misery."

"The time you had with your wife was not miserable, was it Tim?" asked Scrooge.

"Of course not," replied Tim.

"But you managed to go on, and even after the heartbreaking death of your son and daughter in law, you still went on. Correct, Timothy? You weren't miserable, even at that," the spirit reminded him.

"There was a reason then! I had to go on for Luke!" Timothy protested. Then he was more resigned. "There is no reason now. Luke's gone. They're all gone."

For a few moments, no one spoke at all. Finally, it was Timothy who broke the silence. "Well, Spirit, you've shown me a lot. But can you show me one reason for me to continue with my life."

The spirit and Scrooge remained solemnly silent. Tim managed a chuckle. "As I thought. You can't tell me a reason, can you?

"I cannot," answered the spirit. "Which reminds me that it is time that I must be going."

As if ashamed of his sharp tongue, Cratchit stammered in his usual good-natured manner, "Forgive me, Spirit, but I had no intention of offending you. Please stay as long as you wish."

Scrooge answered, as if the spirit was unable to speak for itself, "It is not the job of this spirit to show you what may still be, and yes, he must be going."

Noticing an anguished look on the face of the spirit, Cratchit asked, "Well, why does he look so sad?"

"He is fully aware that if the next spirit is unable to convince you of your worthiness, then there will be no new pasts made-that for you and for the Ghost of Christmas In Your Heart will have no further interludes."

Cratchit watched in amazement as the corpulent ghost vanished before his eyes, its face still contorted in sadness.

"I didn't mean to hurt his feelings," Cratchit said sincerely.

"I know that, Tim. You've never meant to hurt anyone," Scrooge said. "Let's go back to your home and wait for the next spirit- the most important one- the Ghost of Christmas That May Still Be.

## Stave Five - The Christmases That May Still Be

It was nearly 2 am Christmas morning, and Timothy Cratchit sat more soberly than he had the entire evening. His expression remained solemn as he hunkered on the sofa while Ebeneezer Scrooge stood near the tree.

"Tim, my boy, you've lived a virtuous life. You have nothing to fear of the spirits of Christmas!" Scrooge explained paternally.

"Nor have I anything to gain from them," Cratchit retorted more resolute than ever.

"They've convinced me further of what I already know all too well. They've shown me that my life is over. That what I've lived and loved is gone. There is nothing left for me on this plane. It's time for me to move on."

Scrooge sat beside him and thought a moment with his hands supporting his cheeks. "There were certainly times, Tim, before 1843 when I would have moved out of this world. Unlike you, however, I feared the after world and everything else for that matter. In fact, most everything I did had its roots in fear. I loved money, because I feared poverty. I shunned love because I feared rejection. I thought

I hated people because I feared losing them. The opposite of love, my boy, is not hate; it's fear. And in you tonight, you were expressing love's opposite. Not hate, mind you, but you were expressing fear."

"I'm not afraid of death!" exclaimed Cratchit.

"But you have grown afraid of life!" Scrooge explained.

"I've lived a long time! I've stared death and adversity in the face. But now, I wish it all to end. I want it all terminate!" Cratchit proclaimed.

" There is love left in your heart! Why won't you let it out?" Scrooge asked patiently.

"Because I don't want any more pain." He looked directly at Scrooge. "Yes, Uncle Ebeneezer. I am afraid. The world is at war! Never in the history of humankind has the world been in such turmoil-never on this scale. All living relatives that I had upon this continent are gone, and I certainly cannot travel abroad with the world at war." He looked deep into Scrooge's eyes and delineated the words, "I am an old man."

Scrooge cradled the elderly man in his arms as if he were a child. He lead the old man out of doors and onto the porch that showed the now sleeping Cincinnati neighborhood that still awaited Christmas morn- even in this war torn era. "Look around you, Tim. It's Christmas. What was it Fred said? 'The only time I know of, in the long calendar of the year when men and women seem by one consent to open their shut up hearts.'"

"I have never meant to close up my heart. I am in pain." Cratchit conceded.

"Don't let this war win! You feel pain! You've experienced loss, but let your love flow! That's the only way to beat this scourge of a war!" Scrooge looked skyward. "Look at the heaven above us. It bends to encompass the entire globe! It covers America and England! Germany, too. And all the nations. The sky is love. It encircles all and is above all, but we must fix our gaze upward in a positive direction if we are to see it."

Timothy Cratchit and Ebeneezer Scrooge stood arm and arm looking at the still dark sky of pre-dawn Christmas morn, when by appearances it would seem that one particular star approached them, gradually at first, but it became more and more distinct until it cast a great light upon them. Within moments, the being of light stood directly before them. The luminous nature of the entity was such that it was impossible to view it without covering the eyes. Timothy Cratchit only got an occasional glimpse of a face, which at times was a handsome youthful face, but could instantly change to a grotesque countenance with wild contortions and hideous folds of flesh.

A moment passed in silence until finally Timothy broke the stillness. "What is this? What meaning has this for me or anyone else?"

A voice spoke in a calm gentle masculine manner that did not seem to come from either face, but from the encircling heaven above them. "This is the Ghost of Christmas That May Still Be. This is a most ambiguous ghost for there is no way to tell which way each event will unfold. Observe, Timothy Cratchit, and learn what you will."

Timothy Cratchit spoke directly to Ebeneezer Scrooge, who was still standing beside him. "This is the most unpredictable of the ghosts. True?" he asked.

Scrooge answered, "True. Unlike what might have been, these events still may be. And just as we are sure of what is in your heart, we are equally unsure of what will be."

"Then I am sure that I do not to visit with this spirit. I have no interest in what may still be. The future gets here soon enough, and as I've stated throughout this evening, I'm on my way out. I think that I've lived all that I need to and certainly all that I desire to."

Scrooge smiled, "Precisely the reason why you must accompany this spirit to the Christmases that may still be."

The words had barely fallen from Scrooge's lips when the light of the spirit brightened the sky to the point of momentarily blinding Cratchit. The illumination encompassed all that Cratchit could see and when at last he could determine his whereabouts, he realized he was standing precisely where he had been when Scrooge first led him out the door to look at the sky moments earlier. A gray December day found the surroundings of Cratchit's Cincinnati exactly as he knew them in the present.

The spirit still flashed indistinctly, alternating between the dreadful and the pleasant while Scrooge wore a serious mien, though no less pleasant. Cratchit turned to Scrooge and flashed a wordless question.

When at last he spoke, he began, "I know where we are, sure enough. What time is it?"

" A few hours from your present time. It's Christmas. It's 1917. About 11 a.m.," Scrooge answered in a most matter of fact style. Turning suddenly, looking Cratchit directly in the eye, and speaking with the harshness of a reprimanding father, Scrooge added, "And Timothy Robert Cratchit is dead!"

But this stern announcement got little reaction from Timothy Cratchit. After all, death was the only thing he had consistently decided upon as a wish since Luke's demise-at least this was the only wish that he felt he could realistically have honored. After a moment, Cratchit spoke, "Then it's natural. I've never considered taking my own life, so it's what was meant to be."

"Is it?" asked Scrooge. The spirit now was more hideous looking than ever and its former occasional handsome qualities were replaced by consistent ugliness. "As you will see, Timothy, life hinges on the actions of all inhabitants of the earth. We must let love begin within ourselves. Let us see what course of events will follow your death on this particular day."

Opening the front door of the manor, Scrooge motioned as the spirit and Cratchit made their way into the house.

On a sofa in the parlor sat Elsie, crying as her husband, Benjamin tried to comfort her.

"There wasn't anybody here for him! Nobody at all! And then he died all alone on Christmas Eve!" she wailed as her husband soothed her.

"He's with his boy now, and his grandson! That's what he wanted more than anything," Benjamin said.

Turning to Scrooge, unheard by the inhabitants of the future, Cratchit said, "Ben's right! That was my desire. And it must have been the will of God, too."

"Oh Timothy," Scrooge began, "on the journey of life, your eighty-one years are but a grain of sand in the hour glass of time. But if your work on this earth is left unfinished it could take many grains to catch up to the duties left undone by you. For not only does your work get left unattended, but idleness brings misery."

As Scrooge spoke sharply on the last words, the Ghost of Christmas That May Still Be appeared to age many years, wrinkling and withering to become even more unsightly still.

Dr. Strauss entered the parlor quietly. The physician spoke softly, "It is as you expected. He died in his sleep. Most likely a heart attack. Of course, I have seen that when patients loose their will to live, as Mr. Cratchit certainly had, they tend to go quickly. I feel that's what has happened here."

Rumbling footsteps and moving of objects from the porch invaded the solemn air of the house where death had visited. Elsie stood up, looked about, and announced, "No doubt, it's the folks from the mortuary. I had Nathaniel notify them." She walked to the parlor door, looked out to see that her suspicions had proven correct.

Opening the door, two somber men dressed in black carried in a stretcher covered in a white sheet. One asked formally, but knowingly, "Timothy Robert Cratchit estate?"

"Yes, sir," came Elsie's quiet reply.

Dr. Strauss spoke up. "I've signed the certificate of death. Everything is in order and the body is ready to be moved."

The older of the two men stopped cold and gazed directly at the Strauss. His face fixed hard and icy upon the doctor. Finally, he growled, "You're Strauss, aren't you?"

"Dr. Alex Strauss. Yes, I am he." The doctor stood nervously, uncertain of what was happening, but sure that something was erring.

The man turned to Elsie, and asked coldly, "What the hell is he doing here? Damn German probably killed the old man hoping he was in his will."

"Dr. Strauss has been Mr. Cratchit's physician for twelve years," replied Elsie, adamant and devoid of emotion.

"Well, the old man's dead now," said the younger of the two attendants. "I don't suppose anyone needs you now, Strauss. Guess it would be best if you get on out of here and let Doc Johnson sign the 'bill o' sale', so to speak."

"You will have respect for the departed. And you will have respect for Dr. Strauss when you are in this house," Elsie stated, standing up to the larger, younger man who had most recently spoken.

The older attendant stepped forward. "My, aren't you an uppity one!" he commented.

"An uppity what?" Benjamin asked, standing towering over both men. At that moment, Nathaniel walked in and stood beside his father.

"I want you out of here!" Elsie commanded.

"We'll be getting about our business," said the older man in a lowered voice reflecting his change of heart at causing trouble for the doctor.

"Get out of here!" she demanded. "You're not fit to touch Timothy Cratchit, dead or alive! No, get out!"

"You can't just leave a corpse laying in here. You'll be lucky to get anyone else out, it being Christmas Day and all," the younger man explained.

"I believe my mother asked you to leave," Nathaniel reminded them.

Reluctantly, the men made an exit carrying a still empty stretcher. Making their way past the doctor and through the door, Dr. Strauss gained his composure and resumed business proceedings.

"I certainly appreciate you standing up for me," Dr. Strauss noted, "but we still have to properly take care of Mr. Cratchit's body."

"Dr. Strauss, if you will go start up Mr. Cratchit's automobile, Nathaniel and Benjamin will carry Mr. Cratchit out. We'll handle this ourselves," Elsie affirmed.


Timothy Cratchit looked at Scrooge and the still repulsive looking spirit. "I suppose my timing could have been better. I would have preferred they not have had to deal with this on Christmas Day, but they'll all be all right. My will is going to take good care of them. Dr. Strauss will be able to move into another area like he wants where prejudice doesn't run so high. Elsie and Benjamin can move into my home and will live comfortably. That's all there is. I am content."

Scrooge stood silently, the spirit motionless at his side.

"What?" Cratchit began, responding to the silence. "I still don't see the point. You tell me that I've done right by mankind, and I've fulfilled my obligations to my loved ones. So why won't you just let me rest in peace?"

Looking straight ahead, Scrooge began, "While man is on Earth, it is not for him to know what tasks lay before him, or even how numerous those tasks may be. The newborn baby who enters life today may complete his purpose in a day, maybe in twenty years, maybe a hundred. But if he gives up when there are still tasks for him, then there is still good that is left undone. And if it can't come forth from him, the misery caused by the idleness will multiply."

No more had Scrooge uttered these words than the degree of horror upon the appearance of the spirit intensified. Cratchit looked away not wanting to see anymore, but soon found himself in a time and place unfamiliar to him.

Motor cars whizzed by at a speed unbelievably fast. The vehicles were all green and brown- earth tones. Cratchit detected that he was in the middle of some kind of military operation and the modes of transportation around him were unlike anything that he had ever seen or even imagined.

Looking around at the geographical features, he observed aloud, "I am in Europe, correct?"

"Germany, to be precise. Christmas, 1943," answered Scrooge.

Cratchit looked dejected. "This damned old war has gone on forever, hasn't it?"

"Perhaps, it has. Or perhaps it is another war that followed the Great War of your day. Perhaps it is a *more devastating* one! Differences unsettled fester. But if only one voice speaks against the futility of war…"

"I am one old man."

"The journey of a thousand miles starts with a step. You were one man who fed starving orphans. I was one man who allowed you to become a wealthy man instead of a dead child. You are a being of light, a child of God. But if your light ceases to shine, this may be what is to become of your world."

"Why are we here? Why have you brought me to Germany?" asked Cratchit.

"Living in Germany, serving in the German army right now in your time-1917-is a demented young man. A young man who is filled with fear. And he is going to act on that fear. The young man's name is Adolph Hitler." He paused. "Of course, that name means nothing to you, does it?"

Cratchit thought briefly and shrugged, shaking his head. "It does not. I don't know that name."

"Future generations, unfortunately, will not be able to forget that name, and I further regret that it will not be for noble purposes. This man is set on a course that can strike unspeakable atrocities," Scrooge explained. "He'll kill millions."

"And you want me to stop him, Uncle Ebeneezer?" Cratchit asked, taking on a child like air.

"Oh yes, Timothy, I do. I do. But I need your voice and millions of others to stop what has been set in motion. But you can start. You can set things in motion."

"How? How can I do this?" implored Cratchit earnestly.

"Watch. Do you see that man?" asked Scrooge. He pointed to a pale man with short dark hair and a spot of a mustache. A strange configuration of lines on a band adorned the arm of the man's uniform.

"Yes."

"That is he. Adolph Hitler."

"I'm sure that I don't know him," commented Cratchit, failing to see any relevance.

"Look closely at the men around him," Scrooge commanded firmly.

Cratchit eyed the men one by one. Most were young or middle aged officers, but he continued to survey them visually as he had been instructed. Finally, he came to a short, bald man with spectacles. Though more advanced in years than most of the gentleman, he obviously possessed membership to this inner circle. Cratchit realized that the man in the presence and company of Adolph Hitler, the creature that Scrooge said was destined to annihilate millions, was none other than an elderly Dr. Alex Strauss.

"What year did you say it was, Uncle Ebeneezer?"

"1943."

"But that's impossible. Strauss has been in America for years, and he likes it here. Or at least he did, before all this war business with Germany. But surely he would not have been so disenchanted with America to the point that he would turn criminal. He's a good man," Cratchit said, defending his physician.

"Disillusioned is what I'd call it. Strauss has always been on the edge."

Cratchit looked at Scrooge, surprised.

Scrooge continued, "Oh, I'm sure you never saw it. He's been on the straight and narrow with you. He respects you. But with your death, his ridicule increased, and without your guidance his dissatisfaction with America increased, as did his hatred. A hatred of all people unlike himself consumed him to the point that he helped Adolph Hitler commit genocide.

"No, say it's not true," Cratchit pleaded.

"It need not be. But at this point, it may be," Scrooge explained.

At that moment, Timothy Cratchit glanced at the Spirit of Christmas that May Still Be and realized that the intensity of its visual offensiveness had reached what surely had to be its peak.

"Take me away from here! Take me home! I don't want to see anymore!" Cratchit protested.

Scrooge put his hand on the old man's shoulder. "These things need not be. But it is necessary that you observe the things that may still be, not matter how dreadful they are. We still have some time left."

All at once, the scene in which they inhabited went totally black, and Cratchit observed himself in the cool night air. He seemed to sense that he was back in a familiar area. As the landscape lightened, he realized that he was standing on the sidewalk in front of his stately Cincinnati manor house. It looked only slightly different than he remembered it, aged perhaps.

"This is my house," Cratchit observed.

"Not anymore, Timothy. You died in 1917. This is Cincinnati, 1923. It's three days before Christmas. This is Elsie and Benjamin's home now."

"Christmas? Impossible, Elsie always decked this place out. Look at it, it's drab out here. Can we go inside?" Cratchit asked.

"Of course," Scrooge assured him. And transported by an unseen means, they were inside.

Elsie was seated in the parlor. Tears stained her face and her body convulsed in sorrow. In the next room, her husband Benjamin sat at a table, downing the last of his bottle of bourbon whiskey.

Involuntarily, Timothy Cratchit rushed to her. He reached to touch her, but he found himself unable to get near her, held by some invisible force.

"You can't help her, son. You're not even here. You died six years ago," Scrooge reminded him.

"What ever is the matter with her then?" asked Cratchit.

"She's suffered a great loss. A most devastating, worthless loss! She's lost Nathaniel, her son."

"In war?"

"No, not a declared one, anyway," Scrooge explained. "You are keenly aware that racism exists, I know. I am afraid that you were not aware of just how prevalent it was in your own city."

"In Cincinnati? Yes, prejudice exists here, and recently it has gotten worse due to this war, but the blacks have always enjoyed a certain degree of liberty here, certainly more than the South afforded them."

"True, but after your death, things did worsen. You weren't there anymore," Scrooge pointed out.

"One voice! That's all I ever was! I practiced love for all my fellow men, but I wasn't guilty of preaching it! Perhaps I should have!"

"Maybe you should have, Tim," Scrooge assured him, "but never underestimate the value of one virtuous example."

Tim changed the subject. "But what about Benjamin and Elsie? And Nathaniel? What happened to him?"

He handed him a copy of *The Cincinnati Enquirer*. "Here," Scrooge said, "Read all about it." He pointed to an article on the front page. It read:

**Brown Sentenced to be Executed**

Convicted murderer Nathaniel Brown, 24, was sentenced to death by Judge Jonathan Williams in Hamilton County Common Pleas court yesterday afternoon. Last week, Brown, a Cincinnati Negro, was convicted in the race riot murder of four white men outside a downtown tavern in September. Killed in the incident were Kenneth Burchett, 27, Andrew Ruffin, 25, William Brewer,

25, and Daniel Darby, 21. Nine Negroes were also killed in the brawl, but no one has been charged in those deaths yet according to Cincinnati police.

The courtroom scene stood in stark contrast to the jubilant crowd who cheered last week when Brown was convicted. Judge Williams had threatened to hold anyone making a disturbance during yesterday's proceedings. After Williams pronounced the death sentence, only Brown's mother, Elsie Brown, made any vocal utterances, crying aloud as Judge Williams banged his gavel to silence her. Benjamin Brown, the condemned man's father, escorted her from the courtroom.

Nathaniel Brown is scheduled to go to the gallows on January 9, 1924.


Cratchit put the paper down. "How could this happen?" he asked.

Scrooge sighed and stroked his forehead. "After your death, Nathaniel grew up. He saw great injustices for blacks. He knew only a few white people, and now that you were gone, he had none that he admired. He grew very angry. And bitter. He didn't start a lot of trouble, but felt he had nothing to lose. The fact is Tim, he didn't kill all those men, and he didn't kill any of them intentionally. He was just defending his friends, some of whom would instigate trouble."

"Oh Nathaniel, you are so intelligent. How could it have come to this?" Cratchit asked. "And Elsie, dear, dear Elsie. What is to become of you? Tell me, Uncle Ebeneezer...Spirit That may Be, show me another way. Tell me that this won't happen. Is there nothing I can do to change it?"

"Change the action of others? No. We can only influence. We cannot dictate what others will do, even under the best of circumstances, but I believe I hear you telling me that there is more that you want to do."

"I want to help Elsie and her family, and Dr. Strauss, too. But what can I do?"

"My boy, you have already demonstrated to the universe your ability to do the right thing, and the earth still has claim over you. Just go back and fulfill your destiny. You're not finished yet."

"But eighty-one years is a long time," Cratchit said earnestly.

"Bah!" said Scrooge. "Humbug!" And then he laughed. "Come with me, and I'll show a better Christmas yet that may still be."

He looked around at the Spirit as its hideousness faded into a flickering of multi-colored lights. Suddenly, its illumination grew most resplendent and Cratchit again found himself unable to see anything.

Closing his eyes from the glare, Cratchit felt himself moving backward in time and space from where he had been. Upon opening his eyes and gazing around him, he recognized that he was once again in his home, but this time in the vaulted great room which was lavishly decorated for Christmas. Cratchit saw himself, gaily dressed in a white ruffled shirt adorned with a red velvet vest. Elsie entered also dressed in fineries, outfitted in a fine seasonably fashionable dress, which gave her the appearance of Mrs. Santa Claus. Benjamin Brown followed his wife into the room, escorting in caterers and greeting some of Cratchit's employees and other folks with whom he had business dealings. Dr. and Mrs. Strauss were among the guests helping themselves to sandwiches and vegetables.

Elsie jumped up and squealed with delight when she saw a young and pretty African American girl walk in carrying a bundle that was unmistakably a baby. Nathaniel, smartly dressed and smiling, entered carrying assorted baby items. Elsie made her way to them, relieving the young lady of the baby. She doted over the child and caught the attention of Mr. Timothy Cratchit, eighty-seven years old. Elsie, Nathaniel, and his young wife took the baby for the old man's inspection.

"Well, now, what have we here?" Tim asked.

"This is Benjamin Timothy Brown," replied Elsie.

"Named after his Grandpa, and his Uncle Timothy Cratchit," said Nathaniel, continuing his mother's sentence.

"Nathaniel, you and Beverly have paid homage to me in a way that I thought would no longer be possible, especially after my only grandson died. You have truly honored me, and I am grateful." He held the baby.

"He's going to be a fighter!" proclaimed Nathaniel. "Not a physical fighter, but I'm going to show him how to go out and make the world the way it should be."

Beverly smiled. "Why Nate, he's only a month old, and here you are determining his future!" she laughed.

Elsie added, "But he will live in a time better than these, because you and Nathaniel are going to make it better. Just like I fought to do. And Mr. Cratchit fought to do-in Cincinnati and in London, England."

Cratchit added, " And like my mother and father- and Mr. Ebeneezer Scrooge."

The visiting Cratchit looked at Ebeneezer Scrooge and the two shared a smile.

The Ghost of Christmas That May Still Be glowed handsomely, and its facial features became more distinct. It still faded in and out of clarity as Scrooge began to speak.

"Yes, Timothy, the work of man will go on. When your body dies, your work continues through the lives you've touched. But Timothy, the universe still wants you. You still have lives to touch. And someday Tim, the lives that you influence will touch future lives until one Christmas morning all the world will truly be able to proclaim, "Peace on Earth, Goodwill to all its inhabitants!"

Cratchit looked at Scrooge and the two embraced.

"My times grows short," Scrooge whispered.

"Thank you for coming back. Even if this is only a dream, it has been a great comfort to me."

Scrooge looked at Tim. "A dream is real, Timothy. Only, it is experienced in another realm, but a real one, nonetheless."

Cratchit nodded. Looking past Scrooge, the spirit that forever had been changing, caught his eye. He thought he heard Scrooge saying something about a gift, but he could not be sure. His eyes were fixed on this ghost that was now taking a clear, distinct form: it had a handsome youthful face and golden blonde hair.

"Luke!" Cratchit gasped.

It was beyond all doubt the essence of Timothy Cratchit's beloved grandson, bathed in celestial light and surely not of this earth, but still the Luke that the old man dearly loved. For many moments, no words were spoken as the two smiled and gazed at one another. Neither Cratchit nor the boy had ever been more radiant.

Timothy Cratchit cried happily with tears on his cheeks, "Luke, son, I miss you, boy!"

Without speaking, the boy gave only a reassuring smile of pure bliss, pure peace, and unconditional love.

"I know that you've got your things to do wherever you are, and I've learned tonight that I've got duties to tend to. But, we're going to be together again. I know that now!" Cratchit proclaimed.

The youth only nodded, but in that nod, no more loving words were ever spoken.

"Merry Christmas, Luke. I love you," Timothy Cratchit said.

The being of his grandson mouthed words and Cratchit faintly heard the vocalization in Luke's distinguished voice, "I love you, Grandfather! Merry Christmas. Merry Christmas."

Cratchit watched as the being of Christmas That May Still Be, in the form of his grandson, grew brighter and brighter until everything became engulfed in white light. Finally Cratchit saw nothing at all.

## Stave Six - Conclusion

Dawn peeped through the windows of Timothy Cratchit's parlor causing the old man to open his eyes. He peered around the room and down the length of himself, which was reclined on the sofa, he then realized that he had spent the night outside of his bedroom and had not even changed into his nightclothes. He stopped a moment, realizing the events that had just transpired. Then he found himself in the standard melodramatic dilemma, so common in literature and theater, of bewilderment as to whether or not the incidents in his memory were actual facts or a lavish, fantastic dream.

Rising, he replayed every event in his mind. Ebeneezer Scrooge, the spirits of Christmas, and his cherished Luke seemed to be with him on this Christmas morning, as real now as they had been that night. He remembered what each spirit had shown him, the kind, advising words of Ebeneezer Scrooge, and Luke's encouragement for his continuance. It certainly was true. The spirits of the departed were with him as much in his present moment-right here on this Christmas morning- as they had been on the previous night or at any other time on earth. For the first time in many months, Timothy Robert Cratchit felt content.

As he arose, though he had passed the night on the sofa, he felt remarkably rested, which took him to wondering again if he had passed the night on the sofa at all. Perhaps the sofa served only as his landing strip from another dimension. Whatever it was, Cratchit realized that it made no difference whatsoever. The events that he had experienced were real. Nothing had ever been more genuine.

He strolled to the window and looked out where hours earlier he had stood with Ebeneezer Scrooge. "Thank you, Uncle Ebeneezer, thank you so much. Talking to Luke again was more of a gift than I ever expected to be afforded. I'm grateful."

Tears rolled from his eyes. "Thank you, Spirits. You are messengers of God-beings of light. I can't thank you enough. And Luke. Luke, my boy, how I love you so. It's good to know that you're always with me. And that we'll always be together on one plane or another. I think that I already knew that, but it was so kind of you to remind me. And necessary, too, I suppose. I'd given up. I had lost my parents, your parents, Uncle Ebeneezer, but I never dreamed that I'd have to let you go. But it's good to know that you're really here-in my heart- always near me."

Turning from the window, he picked up a photo of Luke that rested on the mantel. "As you know, I've been reminded that my work on Earth is not over. I've still got things to do. And so, Luke, I bid you a 'Merry Christmas' as I prepare for the work I must do today."

Smiling, he sat the picture down and proceeded to his dressing room. He hummed a verse of "Joy to the World" as he readied himself for his departure.

He left the house and began walking toward the back of his house where his Model-A awaited him. He could drive, although usually he had Sloane do the honors. But having given the staff the day off, he managed to prepare the vehicle to start himself. For December 25, the weather kept a mild flavor, neither warm nor cool. As he got in the car, and pulled onto the street, he saw Dr. and Mrs. Strauss, walking along the brick path that lined the street. Dr. Strauss looked up, and quickly looked back. Quickly realizing who was in the horseless carriage, the doctor did not want to acknowledge him in public where someone might see them communicate. That thought, however, was being ignored in the mind of Timothy Cratchit.

He called to them, "Good morning. Merry Christmas to you both!"

"Merry Christmas," uttered the couple in a low, unemotional voice.

"Isn't it a glorious morning?" called Cratchit out to them. "Sure it's a little chilly out here, but it's Christmas and it's good to be alive! Where are you headed?"

Dr. Strauss looked at his wife and then glanced up and down the street. He took his wife by the arm and briskly walked up to Mr. Cratchit's automobile.

"Good morning, Mr. Cratchit. Merry Christmas, sir," said Dr. Strauss.

"Merry Christmas," Mrs. Strauss repeated.

"Where are you two off to this fine Christmas morning?" asked Cratchit cheerfully.

Still glancing over his shoulder, Dr. Strauss ignored the question and warned, "Mr. Cratchit, today it is Christmas. But tomorrow will be just another day and you and I both live in this city. Need I remind you that our roots are in different parts of Europe and on different sides of the war."

"Drivel!" muttered Cratchit. "Now, are you going to Christmas services?

"Yes, we're headed to the New Thought Temple," Mrs. Strauss answered.

Cratchit smiled. " The one on East McMillan? That's where I'm headed- a great place to feed the soul and Christmas services have always been my favorite ones. Hop in and we'll ride together."

"Mr. Cratchit, we mustn't impose," Dr. Strauss rebutted.

"What imposition?" protested Cratchit. "That's where I am headed."

The doctor tensed his lips. "Mr. Cratchit, Christmas or not, it is not advisable for us to be seen together."

"Are we not of the same human race? Do we not both adore goodness and deplore evil? No, I insist that you ride with me over to the square, and I shall proudly accompany you into Christmas services. I'll have it no other way," Cratchit responded.

The couple stood next to the car, and seeing the determination that the old man possessed, they decided it may be less causing of a scene to simply board the automobile and quietly enter the church. Hesitantly, they embarked upon the vehicle and, once secure inside, Cratchit steered the automobile around a corner and down the street.

"You are my physician and my friend. I erred in acting any other manner. It doesn't matter from what race or nationality a person brings his personage! We are all in this human race together," Cratchit stated firmly.

"Well, I'm afraid your opinion is in the minority view, Mr. Cratchit," Dr. Strauss remarked.

Timothy Cratchit stated firmly, "Minority is not wrong! Think about it. The greatest idea in the world starts in the mind of one man or woman and has to be given time to grow. Many will embrace it someday, but it remains a minority until a critical mass is reached. But remember, there is nothing magic about fifty-one percent! No, minority is not wrong!"

Mr. Cratchit parked the automobile directly in front of the front doors of the church. The grand structure on this winter morning contained all the qualities of a Christmas card. The chiming of the bells filled the air as Cratchit and the Strausses exited the vehicle and walked into the church.

Candles lit the sanctuary and the quiet and peace that pervaded the arena gave no hint of the Great War that was being fought an ocean away. The trio found a seat in a pew midway through the church that found itself more full than usual due to the holiday. As they sat, Mrs. Strauss helped Timothy Cratchit take his wrap off as Dr. Strauss looked at the octogenarian. All the while, "O Holy Night" played beautifully from the church organ.

When at last they were settled in, Dr. Strauss whispered, "Yesterday, you made it quite clear that you would be spending Christmas at home. I'm surprised to see you. And equally surprised that you gave us a ride given the differences in our heritage. Let me remind you that there is a war going on and that this is Cincinnati. It's not exactly fond of being the "city of immigrants" these days."

"It needs to be proud that all who come here do so. No matter what the creed or customs they bring with them," Cratchit said.

At last the sound of the organ reached crescendo and the choir stood, delivering a splendid verse of "Joy to the World." Cratchit glowed with joy in his world for he had never felt such glee in all of his life.

When the sounding joy was repeated and completed with the next stanzas, the choir sat down and the minister arose. Possessing a kind face and a tall slender build, the clergyman ascended to the podium and announced, "Merry Christmas." But in those two words came an outpouring from the depths of man that was evident to all. There was no cliché in those two words that he spoke, no matter how many times they had been uttered before.

He looked around the church and into the faces of the congregates. "Welcome to this place of sanctuary. We are told and many of us know all too well that we are engaged in a Great War of the World. There has been much talk of the need to downplay the celebrations of Christmas this year. And I did entertain that thought myself early in the season."

Cratchit's expression changed and grew uneasy momentarily, remembering the feeling that the minister was describing all too well. Nonetheless, he quickly returned his thoughts to the present moment.

"But is there not enough gloom and regret in the world?" the minister asked. "Shouldn't we look for joy, even if it is not openly present to us? Is "Joy to the World" just a song we sing, or do we mean it?"

"When we sing that precious carol and proclaim joy to the world, we are claiming that for all the world, not just the faction of the world that agrees with us. And as we celebrate in our own faith, there are countless other celebrations of renewal going on throughout the world. In our own beloved city of Cincinnati and throughout the world, our Jewish brethren are commencing their celebration of the miracle of light. In a little more than a month, the Chinese will be observing their New Year, a time for spiritual purging of the old and rebirth. And here in Christendom, we celebrate what we call Christmas. We observe the birth of a humble child and are reminded of our own origins and that we, too, can rise to great heights."

"And so it would appear that we all have the right idea. Love and renewal- and casting off of the old and an embracing of the new. But yet, we find ourselves and the world at war. So do we simply cast aside the good will we have proclaimed during past Christmases and succumb to the misery of destruction?

Half a century ago, this land found itself in the midst of the Civil War. During that destructive opus of American history, the poet Henry Wadsworth Longfellow wrote these words upon hearing the bells of Christmas:

> And in despair, I bowed my head
> There is no peace on Earth, I said.
> For hate is strong and mocks the song,
> Of peace on Earth, goodwill to men!"

"And then, the poet reminds us of the insights that can sometimes be spoken to us only in moments of true reflection. So often, these insights do not come to us in words, but as in instantaneous thought. He wrote:

> Then pealed the bells more loud and sweet,
> "God is not dead, nor does he sleep,
> The wrong shall fail, the right prevail
> With peace on Earth, goodwill to men!"

"Nothing lasts forever, save love! This war will end. Let it end with us now-at this moment! Let us embrace all! The Prayer of St. Francis of Assissi states:

> Lord, make me an instrument of your peace.
> Where there is hatred.....let me sow love.
> Where there is injury.....pardon.

> Where there is doubt.......faith.
> Where there is despair......hope.
> Where there is darkness........light.
> Where there is sadness.........joy.
> Oh Divine Master, grant that I may not so much seek to be consoled...as to console.
> To be understood...as to understand.
> To be loved....as to love.
> For it is in giving that we receive.
> It is pardoning that we are pardoned.
> It is in dying that we are born to eternal life.

He paused, reflectively. "I have asked the choir to perform a song that I last heard them do on Christmas Day, 1913. It was written by German composer, Gregor Handel as part of his program, *The Messiah.*"

Instantly, upon a signal given by the director, the pipe organ thundered the introduction to Handel's "Hallelujah". The choir rose and proclaimed the anthem! The mood of the church was triumphant, and Timothy Cratchit and the Strausses embraced.

They each spoke Christmas greetings as joy filled the sanctuary.

The hour was nearing 11 a.m. as Timothy Cratchit maneuvered the Model A in front of the home of Benjamin and Elsie Brown. Their eldest son, Nathaniel, walked out toward the automobile to assist the old man. The handsome youth smiled as the old man turned to exit the vehicle. Their eyes met and they held the gaze.

Seemingly out of nowhere, Timothy Cratchit asked, "Nathaniel, do you like working with numbers?"

The boy was genuinely puzzled. "Mathematics is my best subject in school, sir," Nathaniel responded.

"A bright boy, that I can tell you are. You know, I recently lost my grandson to the war. I had always thought he would run my business. But with him gone, and my son and daughter-in-law both passed on as well, I'm without anyone to pass my legacy to stateside. My Family in Europe is pretty much content to stay there. I was wondering if you might not start stopping by the office after school."

"Oh yes, sir," Nathaniel proclaimed, realizing what he was being offered.

"If you work hard, there will be a lot of success come your way, I can guarantee you that!" Cratchit stated. "Now, I believe I smell some your mother's Christmas magic coming from the kitchen, and if I can smell it out here, then we best get inside before it attracts the whole neighborhood."

They smiled. Arm in arm, aged and youth-white and black, strode into the home.

Having finished the Christmas feast, Elsie and Benjamin's four children along with the adults sat at the table as Cratchit reflected on the sermon that he had heard this morning. While he did so, the Browns were occupied with chatter, until finally Elsie spoke up. "Mr. Cratchit? Are you all right?"

He smiled. "I'm more than all right. It's just sometimes, I need a little reminding of that."

Changing the subject, he asked, " Did Nathaniel tell you of our agreement that we made this morning?"

"Yes, he did," Benjamin answered enthusiastically. "Thank you for taking an interest in him, Mr. Cratchit."

"Nathaniel has a good head on his shoulders. This is his legacy; a legacy that you and Elsie have earned for him through your service to me. I'll need someone to take over operations. I'm thinking that I won't be around here next Christmas."

The room was silent momentarily.

Elsie began, " Mr. Cratchit, Dr. Strauss says your health is good. There is no reason why you need to think about passing on."

"Passing on?" asked Cratchit. "Who said anything about the grave? I'm not practicing for death! I'm going to visit my family in England!"

It was not until Christmas, 1919 that Timothy Cratchit got to visit his surviving brothers and sisters in England after the war's end. He had an excellent visit, but wanted to return to Cincinnati where he lived until his death at the age of ninety-two in 1928. He never had to see another war, and continued to live out the creed he had spoken in England on Christmas Day so many years earlier, "God Bless Us, Everyone!"

# Why Set A Dickens Sequel in Cincinnati?

As both an educator and an interested scholar, I have spent many hours pouring over the writings of Charles Dickens. While you grow to know a lot about Dickens through his fiction, the author was a bit more plain spoken and no less outspoken in his factual writings in journals, diaries, and correspondence.

Dickens was not particularly fond of America, but he was fascinated with it, choosing to tour it twice in his lifetime. When you consider the modes of transportation of the day, both intercontinental and transcontinental, a voyage from the European continent to North America and back on two occasions was no minor feat. Still Dickens did manage to have positive comments about two major American cities: Boston, Massachusetts and Cincinnati, Ohio.

His first visit to Cincinnati came in 1842, which was one year before he wrote *A Christmas Carol*. During this visit he made many stops in the area that some area businesses can still proudly lay claim to; most notably of these is the Golden Lamb Inn in Lebanon, Ohio which neighbors Cincinnati.

I also chose Cincinnati because the facts fit. The city became a new home to thousands of immigrants in the latter half of the nineteenth century and early twentieth century, and the events that occurred in the story relative to the war are historical fact. (This is one scourge in the city's long history as with every town or city. Of course, there are other blemishes, but Cincinnati is a great place!)

I have tried to write this as Dickens might have had he chosen to do so (and been alive) in 1917. I make no claim to his masterful skills, but I have enjoyed the story of Ebeneezer Scrooge for all of my life, and have long wanted more. Hundreds of adaptations exist, and a few authors have endeavored to put Scrooge into other stories, but to my knowledge, we left Tiny Tim Cratchit a boy of six or seven in 1843. In 1917, Dickens fictional character would have indeed been eighty or eighty-one years old.

**About the author:**

Dale Powell (1962-   )

Dale Powell is a teacher and writer who lives in rural Southern Ohio. He is a middle school teacher, an adjunct professor of English at Shawnee State University, author, part-time paralegal, and workshop presenter. His wife, Barbara, is also a middle school teacher. They have two sons, Nathan and Shawn.

Mr. Powell has independently studied the lives and works of authors Charles Dickens and Edgar Allan Poe and incorporated these subjects into his classroom teaching. Powell's diverse interests include civil rights, metaphysical studies, paranormal studies, American history, rock music, and children's issues.

He is the author of several plays and short stories. *Timothy Cratchit's Christmas Carol, 1917* is his first nationally published novel.